The Shining Trapezonearon
by Robert M. Price

The Reverend Enoch Bowen was already excited at the prospect of traveling to Egypt with an expedition from Miskatonic University. He had won a lottery whereby the Antiquities Department provided one fortunate applicant passage on the trip. It was principally a public gesture to court the good will of New Englanders. For a clergyman to be included in such a dig helped reassure the pious who were easily offended at some of the recent discoveries made in far-flung places like Egypt and Babylon, hieroglyphic and Cuneiform inscriptions that challenged traditional readings of holy scripture. Like many of his colleagues in those days, the Reverend Bowen, while no professional academic, was a well-informed amateur in scholarly questions, especially as regards biblical history, and he was understandably thrilled to see the world of the Bible face to face. He felt the experience would make his faith more real, more vibrant. It was too late to meet Moses or Pharaoh in person, but meeting the eternal sands of Egypt was almost as good.

But his enthusiasm fully blossomed only after a particularly striking dream that visited him the night after he had been informed of his prize. He was quite excited and found it harder than usual to fall asleep. A sleeping draught took care of that, and his dream, as if waiting impatiently for him, descended at once. Mr. Bowen found himself lying, clothed in a linen tunic, on a smoothly tiled floor. He was sure he had never visited the place in waking life. It was cold, though the air was static, unmoved by any hint of a breeze. His slightest movement set off light echoes. It was dimly lit, he thought by bracketed torches, though they did not fall within his field of vision. The light was, he thought, greenish in tint. And then a vague form appeared before him. Strangely, its details were obscured, either because the form was in shadow or because the light was too bright, though a moment before it had seemed so weak. But such illogic and ambiguity were to be expected in dreams. Mr. Bowen found one thing very clear, however, and that was what the figure said to him. The angel, as the pious pastor supposed, told him he must find what was lost to mankind, a great treasure of a spiritual nature. It was a Grail of knowledge for which the world was starved, and God had chosen Mr. Bowen to bring it to light.

When the sleeper awakened, he remembered what had transpired in the dream, which was unusual for him. Did it mean anything? Was it simply a figment of his own prideful self-importance? Or had God really spoken to him? He sat up in bed pondering this for a few minutes, then rolled over and went back to sleep. He didn't quite know how seriously to take the dream, but in the morning he arose with an unshakeable sense of adventurous expectancy.

Mr. Bowen would be away for the whole summer for this sabbatical, and it was a tearful farewell he received from the congregation of the First Free Will Baptist Church of Providence. His sermon on his last Sunday before departure was "Seeking God in the Sands of Egypt," and several congregants shook his hand and told him, sincerely or not, it was one of his best, and he appreciated the compliment. The next morning Mr. Bowen caught the train to Massachusetts, to Arkham Station. A taxi took him the rest of the way to the University, where he was greeted by the chairman of the Department of Antiquities and two of the archaeology professors, one a faculty member at Miskatonic, the other from nearby Harvard. All three seemed generally affable, but Mr. Bowen was a keen observer and thought he detected a hint of condescension. He understood and took no offense. He would take care not to get in the way and to do anything he could to assist the efforts of the experts whom he was privileged to accompany.

He did wish his learned companions would deign to confide more of their plans to him. The little he picked up that evening at a reception implied their goal was to discover the hidden tomb of a half-mythical Pharaoh named Nephren-Ka. That king's successors, the story went, had sought to efface every mention of him from monuments and documents, the same thing that had ensued upon the death of the similarly heretical Akhenaten. Their thoroughness made it especially difficult to track down his relics after so many centuries. The paucity of surviving evidence made most Egyptologists skeptical of the very existence of this Nephren-Ka. Certainly the Reverend Bowen had never heard the name.

Mr. Bowen spent most of the boat trip across the Atlantic, through the Pillars of Hercules, across the Mediterranean, and into Egypt, in intense Bible study and meditation. To what end, he did not quite know. He only knew he returned again and again to the Genesis tale of Joseph in Egypt, how he entered that dusky kingdom as a slave betrayed by his brethren who had grown to resent their father's obvious preference for this brat who boasted of dreams in which his elders bowed before him. No matter the depths into which fate cast Joseph, his gifts were soon recognized by his captors who promoted him to positions of authority and responsibility, until eventually he attained the office of the Pharaoh's Grand Vizier, master of all Egypt in all but name. Mr. Bowen knew the story well and had known it since boyhood. But now he seemed to sense a new depth, a new

Weirdbook

ANNUAL #2

Features

From the Editor's Tower, by Doug Draa. 2

Stories

The Shining Trapezohedron, by Robert M. Price 3

A Noble Endeavor, by Lucy A. Snyder 10

Ancient Astronauts, by Cynthia Ward 24

The Thing in the Pond, by John R. Fultz 34

Enter The Cobweb Queen, by Adrian Cole 42

Tricks No Treats, by Paul Dale Anderson .58

Ronnie and the River, by Christian Riley 65

Cellar Dweller, by Franklyn Searight 72

Yellow Labeled VHS Tape, by R.C. Mulhare .84

Tuama, by L.F. Falconer 95

Mercy Holds No Measure, by Kenneth Bykerk 105

Treacherous Memory, by Glynn Owen Barrass 118

The Hutchison Boy, by Darrell Schweitzer 128

Poetry

Dolmen of The Moon, by Deuce Richardson .23

Lovecraftian Limerick, by Andrew J. Wilson .33

A Wizard's Daughter, by Ann K. Schwader 138

The Shadow of Azathoth is your Galaxy, by DB Spitzer 140

Ascend, by Mark A. Mihalko 141

The Solace of the Farther Moon, by Allan Rozinski 143

The Stars Are Always Right, by Charles Lovecraft 144

Daemonic Nathicana, by K.A. Opperman. 145

Asenath, by Ashley Dioses. 146

The Book of Eibon/Le Livre D'eibon, trans. by Frederick J. Mayer. 147

From the Editor's Tower

We here at *Weirdbook* decided to do a yearly themed fifth issue. An *Annual* if you will.

Last years theme was "Witches" and it turned out to be one of our most popular issues to date. After much soul searching it was decided that this years theme would be the ever popular "Cthulhu Mythos" created by Mr. Howard Phillips Lovecraft, that esteemed gentleman from Providence.

One of the main reasons "The Mythos" was picked was mainly due to its undying popularity. Even after more than 9 decades, Mr. Lovecraft's literary universe still continues to fire the imaginations of both writers and readers alike. It's not an overstatement to say that Mr. Lovecraft's fans and those of his Mythos' are truly legion and beyond numbering.

I think that you, the reader will find this a highly enjoyable issue full of eldritch, unspeakable, and nameless horrors. I decided that this issue should contain stories by the finest of *Weirdbook's* regular contributors. This list includes such luminaries as Lucy A. Snyder, Ann K. Schwader, Leanna Falconer, Cynthia Ward, Darrell Schweitzer, Adrian Cole, and John R. Fultz to name just a few. I'm also very proud to have a brand new story from Mr. Robert M. Price which marks his very first appearance in this incarnation of *Weirdbook*! I can honestly call this **_Weirdbook's_ very first All Star Issue!**

By the time that this issue arrives at your doorstep, the days will have gotten shorter and cooler. I hope that it adds to the thrills and chills that are inherent to the season. So enjoy!

—Doug Draa

Staff

PUBLISHER & EXECUTIVE EDITOR

John Gregory Betancourt

EDITOR

Doug Draa

CONSULTING EDITOR

W. Paul Ganley

WILDSIDE PRESS SUBSCRIPTION SERVICES

Carla Coupe

PRODUCTION TEAM

Steve Coupe
Sam Cooper
Shawn Garrett
Helen McGee
Karl Würf

relevance to his own case.

When he had puzzled over Joseph to the point of frustration, he would turn several pages back to an earlier chapter to focus on the brief but enigmatic anecdote of Enoch, the pre-Flood patriarch who escaped death, being taken up bodily into heaven to walk, like the sun, with God across the heavens. This passage, too, was long familiar to him, as he bore the same name and had, as a young boy, always delighted to see his own name in holy scripture. But now he sensed a deeper significance in the strange episode. At length he closed the book and decided he would let unfolding events make clear the message that attracted but eluded him.

Once the archaeologists had established their camp and negotiated the hire of local workers to do their digging, they spread their maps, drawing perimeters for the first round of excavations. Now the scantiness of evidence came home to them with new force. How little they really had to go on, even to know where to look. Miskatonic Professor Daniel Aiken remarked in exasperation that they might as well flip a coin. Most of his colleagues agreed, but Mr. Bowen kept his silence, unwilling to voice his confidence that guidance would soon be forthcoming, perhaps from God. He knew what the archaeologists would say to that.

The outsider cleric offered to assist in the digging and disposing of the sandy soil, but he was in his sixties and, as a native New Englander unused to such heat, he found even minor efforts quickly exhausting. Professor Aiken and the others forbade further exertions, though Mr. Bowen's efforts seemed to increase their respect for him. Then the Harvard archaeologist, Dr. Alan Farrington, approached him with a welcome suggestion.

"Reverend Bowen, I think I have a special job for you. You're just the man. I have received word from a colleague down south in Abyssinia who has been offered a sheaf of Coptic manuscripts, seemingly of Gnostic provenance. Such offers are far from unique, and many prove to be frauds, a sophisticated version of dummy artifacts manufactured in back room workshops by crafty rogues for sale at exorbitant prices to gullible explorers too eager to make discoveries. My contact asks me to make the trip to consult about the texts, but I just cannot take the time away from our project here, fruitless though it seems so far to be. I wonder if you would make the trip to examine the manuscripts and give an opinion. Of course, if it looks promising, we will take the materials back home, leaving an earnest payment, for final authentication. So we don't expect you to bear the burden of final decision. Sound interesting?"

"Interesting? It sounds exciting! Of course I shall be delighted to help in any way I can!"

* * * *

Though the only means of travel available was a camel, and it was by no means comfortable, the Reverend Bowen could not repress a thrill at the thought of himself riding a camel like a true Bedouin. But this did not last long, for soon he and his guide boarded a boat up the Nile. The old clergyman was seized by new wonderment at the sight of a Monophysite monastery sunk entirely into the dry earth, dug laboriously ages before, a weird counter to the Edomite fortress city of Petra, carved from red sandstone cliffs above ground. As it turned out, the dealer of whom he had been told was actually an agent for the monastery. The monks had decided to part with some of their treasures to ameliorate their chronic financial distress. The old, wizened men seemed relieved that the potential buyer, as they regarded Mr. Bowen, was a fellow "holy man." For his part, Mr. Bowen was equally relieved to know that the manuscripts came directly from a monastic community; since this lessened the likelihood of the codices being fraudulent, though of course pious frauds were hardly unknown. A meeting of the minds was quickly achieved, and Mr. Bowen spent but a single night among the monks.

When he awoke the next morning, he was much surprised, not to say distressed, to discover his guide had disappeared without a word. Asking around, Mr. Bowen found no one who admitted to knowing anything about the man, but he could not help thinking the agent of sale knew something. His anxiety dissipated, however, when the agent offered to accompany him on his return trip. The man surprised him further by suggesting the two of them return to Egypt on camelback, by a different route. He said he knew of an ancient site, as yet unknown to Western archaeologists, and that he suspected the learned American clergyman might enjoy seeing it. The fellow, a native Egyptian, was named Abu Serif, and he did not seem particularly devious. Mr. Bowen knew he might be taking a risk, but against this consideration was his awareness that his completed task of assessing the codices must have been mainly a ploy merely to keep him busy, but that now he might have a golden opportunity to make a real contribution to the expedition. So he shook hands with Abu-Serif and quickly made ready to depart. The monks watched the pair ride off, the barest hint of an equivocal expression on their eternally impassive faces.

The ride through the desert was long and difficult. This time, Mr. Bowen found his stomach churning uncontrollably, so he did not try to converse much with his guide. He would slip intermittently into a half-daze, and it was all he could do to hold onto the saddle of his mount. A pounding, splitting headache cost him any real sense of the passage of time. Finally, they came to a stop, after some days. Mr. Bowen could no longer remember whether they had stopped for food and sleep, or how often. He felt an aching in his middle, but he did not know whether to attribute this to hunger or to nausea. But now he did lie down on a rug for some sleep, as Abu-Serif watched over him. As he yielded to Morpheus, Mr. Bowen imagined he heard the faint sounds of jackals barking in the distance.

As the aching, sun-burned American regained his senses with the morning light, Abu-Serif handed him some dried meat and a soup can of coffee, which he gratefully received. The two exchanged no pleasantries. Suddenly the Egyptian broke the silence and blurted out, "*Sahib* Bowen. It is time I tell you what we seek. Indeed we have reached it now. It is said to be the tomb of *the Black Pharaoh, Nephren-Ka*."

Mr. Bowen's eyes widened and focused as he set aside his meager rations, all hunger forgotten. "The tomb of…. Why, that's exactly what we…"

"Yes, *sahib*. I know who you are and why you have come here. Or shall I say, why you were summoned here."

Ignoring this last bit, which did not register with him as he did not understand it, Mr. Bowen replied, "But why just me? Why not rejoin the expedition and bring the rest of them?"

"The professors are not wanted. You are."

"By whom?"

"Why not ask him yourself? Are you ready?"

Mr. Bowen rose to his feet and followed his enigmatic guide only a short distance to the open mouth of an already exposed tomb entrance. Someone had obviously beaten the Miskatonic expedition to the prize. It was surely odd that the university archaeologists had known nothing of a rival endeavor. But here he was. He supposed that he, too, was beating his colleagues to the prize. How their opinion of this "fifth wheel" would change!

Abu-Serif stood silently to the side of the sandy path down to the open threshold of the tomb, his hand extended in the same direction, like a maitre d at a restaurant. Mr. Bowen felt decidedly awkward at the changed nature of the situation. He did not like being the focus of some staged, planned charade, or even a trap.

* * * *

Professor Aiken was concerned. The Reverend Bowen was long overdue. Dr. Farrington of Harvard had taken a certain liking to the bright clergyman and proposed forming a search party. "I realize it would sidetrack the dig, but we seem to be getting nowhere on that score anyway. I think we stand a better chance of finding a living colleague than a dead Pharaoh."

The next day, the two professors explained the new mission to the native diggers, half of whom took off with them to search for the missing Mr. Bowen. Everyone else half-heartedly continued with their examination of the countryside for any indication of the site they sought.

* * * *

His peripheral vision revealed little as Mr. Bowen paced steadily down a very long, dimly illumined hall. At last, where the hall ended in a chamber perhaps only twice the width of the walkway leading to it, he took note of his destination. His first reaction was one of alarm, even panic, for he saw that he now stood on the same stone-flagged floor he had seen in his dream weeks before. As he recognized more and more details of the chamber, which seemed to be growing lighter, he had both a sense of dread and a kind of relief that the other shoe had finally fallen. He had anticipated *something*, and this had to be it. He knew that, if the dream were to continue unfolding into waking reality, he should momentarily meet the one who had summoned him. He had not long to wait.

"In the Name of Mighty Nyarlatophis."

A three-dimensional silhouette of absolute blackness and radiating cold stood before him. The stone floor and walls had turned to glowing emerald green, which, however, did nothing to illumine the void of speaking shadow. "I am the Trismegistus. Men once called me Pharaoh. Now behold: I am about to do a new thing. I shall make all things new. And you, Enoch, blessed above my Million Favored Ones, shall bring these tidings to mankind who are like sheep without a shepherd."

At this, Mr. Bowen fell prostrate before him, averting his gaze.

"Take this, my beloved. Look into its depths, and you will know as you are known."

It was a strangely cut stone with asymmetrical facets. It glowed softly with an inner, blood-red radiance. Fleeting images shifted within it.

* * * *

He struggled to find light in a black void till all at once his (or someone's) tattered eyelids sprang open to the sight of shadowy conspirators huddled around his sarcophagus. As the strange light of the gem known as the Heart of Ahriman fell upon him, he remembered that his ancient name, unspoken among men for millennia, was Xaltotun.

* * * *

He found himself screaming under torture in the black cyclopean citadel called Beled-el-Djinn, the City of Devils, by some and by others Karashehr, the Black City. His name was Xuthltan, and now he gathered his waning strength to curse the king who tormented him in order to secure his hellfire-red gem, the Fire of Asshurbanipal, which disclosed the secrets of future ages. Blood clouded his eyes as he saw the tentacled devil he had summoned emerging from a writhing shroud of black fog.

* * * *

He watched as Belshazzar, King of Babylon, received the blood-red gem from the hand of a diver who had dredged it up from a forgotten ruin sitting on the seabed of the Persian Gulf, where it had decorated the mossy breast of a mummified king. Time hurtled by as he saw Cyrus seize the jewel from around the fat neck of Belshazzar, from whence it passed from king to king, from thief to thief, always causing its owner to slake its evil thirst with the blood of screaming virgins.

* * * *

He beheld Apollonius of Tyana. He *was* Apollonius of Tyana, whom some deemed a charlatan, others a wizard, still others the son of the god Proteus. He gazed into the Philosopher's Stone of the alchemists and lifted his head filled with new secrets…

* * * *

He saw, as if descending from above, the hunched-over form of Joseph Smith, whose sweating face was buried in a cloth hat, his straining eyes fixed on the glowing Seer Stone that revealed to him the unknown histories of vanished peoples.

* * * *

The desperate search for the straying Mr. Bowen had been more thorough, more expansive, than the search for the tomb of Nephren-Ka, though, had they only known it, they were not so far from the burial place they had sought. The weary archaeologists had regathered, doubly disappointed. It took little discussion for them to decide to cut bait and return to the States. They were very nearly all packed to set off when they were profoundly shocked to behold old Bowen, much changed, walking into the encampment.

The spare figure, standing proudly erect, was burnt black by the desert sun. He was clad in deep red robes, or shreds of them, perhaps foraged from a violated tomb. Two mangy jackals accompanied the man, affectionately licking his outstretched hands. The dusky laborers bowed to him as one man. The Americans, clad in their khakis and pith helmets, knew not what to say, or to think.

A Noble Endeavor
by Lucy A. Snyder

The linen room door slammed open, and Mariette nearly dropped the towel she was folding. She tried to be very still and didn't turn around. The stump of her left knee ached inside the leather cup of her peg leg.

"You!" The plantation foreman Zeke sounded annoyed and worried. "Girl! Go on up to Doc Bronson's lab."

Her heart beat faster and her vision seemed to go dark at the edges. She focused on folding the towel just so. Told herself that it was just the sharp odor of the lye soap that was making tears rise in her eyes. There were four other girls working shoulder to shoulder with her—the Master had seven legitimate children and it took nearly that many slaves to handle all their laundry—so he could have meant any of them. Couldn't he? But deep down she knew that since she was the only girl in the room who still had all her fingers, he had to be calling her out. Dr. Bronson only wanted helpers with good hands.

Oh, Lord, please don't let him mean me, she prayed. *Ain't it enough I lost my leg? I got to lose my mind and my life, too?*

"Girl!" Zeke's huge, calloused hand landed on her shoulder and spun her around. The tip of her peg skidded on the polished floor and she nearly fell.

He glowered down at her, his gray eyes bloodshot from sun and smoke and rum. "You deaf, girl?"

"No sir," she stammered. The other girls were staring at her; she could practically feel their relief like the ocean breeze upon her sweating skin. "I'm sorry. I didn't 'spect you meant me?"

"I do mean you. Get on up to the lab."

"He need fresh linens?" *Please, Lord, let it be that he just needs sheets or a towel or a clean chamber pot.*

"I reckon he probably does, but that damn fool Bo touched something he shouldn't and now what little brains he had are drippin' out his ears."

She froze again. Dr. Bronson's laboratory had only been up on the hill for a year but already six boys had gone in as assistants and been carried out weeks later, stone dead or babbling with madness. Rumor was that Dr. Bronson's research back in London had killed so many working-class apprentices that eventually the boys' grieving parents revolted and burned the laboratory to the ground. Dr. Bronson escaped across the Atlantic with his life and lab books and sought refuge at his cousin's Barbados sugar plantation.

Nobody quite knew what was going on inside the laboratory, nor would Mr. Turner speak of the arrangement he'd made with the scientist. Some folks whispered that Dr. Bronson had promised Mr. Turner tremendous riches if his research succeeded. They said that surely Dr. Bronson was trying to create a Philosopher's stone to turn lead into gold. Others said that Mr. Turner was desperate to save his eldest son Johnny from the dissolution and vicious rages he'd flown into ever since the young man returned from a stint in the British navy. If the doctor had promised a cure, then perhaps he was driving his slave assistants mad on purpose to test remedies for Johnny. But if not…Mariette shuddered.

The foreman cuffed her on the side of her head, making her ear ring painfully. "Quit yer dawdlin' and get up there! If I catch you lollygaggin' I'll take you to Johnny. You want that?"

For a moment, Mariette thought she might faint, but she forced herself to say, "No sir."

Her mind fogged with terror, she moved like one of the clockwork men of Boston as she loaded a set of towels and a fresh set of sheets into a basket and marched out of the linen room. Whatever horrors awaited her in the laboratory, they would be far better than being a plaything for Johnny Turner.

He was the reason she'd lost her leg. After Johnny returned from the navy, his father made him foreman over the family's sugar cane plantation, reasoning that with his military experience his eldest would maintain good order and keep the slaves productive. Mr. Turner didn't mind if his boys satisfied their male urges on female slaves or entertained themselves by thinking up ever-more-gruesome ways of tormenting recaptured runaways. He was fond of saying, "A scared slave is a hard worker. Make them fear you more than they fear God and you'll always have a bountiful crop."

But Mr. Turner was first and foremost a businessman; as much as he figured slaves needed harsh discipline and that his sons needed to blow off a little steam now and then, he'd sunk good money into his slaves and didn't want to see his property damaged without reason. Johnny started carrying a boarding axe he'd kept from his navy days and anytime a slave displeased him, he'd lop off one of their fingers, starting with the pinkie. Some slaves healed up well enough but others got infections and lost hands, arms, even their lives. And the doctoring got expensive. It was Mariette's own crippling that finally made Mr. Turner lock Johnny in his rooms and bring Zeke down from South Carolina to work as his new foreman.

When Mariette was ten, a slave named Tom ran away and was recaptured when he tried to stow away on a ship bound for London. The slave catchers brought him back beaten half to death, but that wasn't good enough for Johnny. He made the slaves build a gibbet in the yard and hung Tom from it by his arms. Then Johnny made the slaves pile dry brush beneath him and light it. He made all the slaves stand in a circle around the gibbet and watch as Tom screamed and slowly burned to death.

Mariette stayed rooted to the spot, but when the flesh started peeling off Tom's feet, she closed her eyes. Johnny noticed her averted gaze and flew into a rage.

"You watch as long as I tell you to watch!" He pulled his Bowie knife from his belt and stabbed the blade through her bare foot into the red dirt.

She remembered the sudden mind-breaking pain, and then everything going black. The days after that were hazy in her memory. She remembered lying on her mother's cot in their tiny coral hut, her mother trying to get her to drink some bitter medicinal draught. Then there was the horror of waking up to find herself strapped to a board, a leather strip in her mouth to keep her from biting off her own tongue or breaking her teeth, and the physician from Bridgetown heating his bone saw in the fire while telling her mother, "Hold her down. This won't take but a minute."

When she finally awoke from the fever, her leg was gone from a few inches below her knee and she was so weak that all she could do was polish silverware in the manor. Her weakness lasted close to a year; Mr. Turner seemed regretful and had his own family physician check on her to make sure her wound healed as well as possible. Mariette was light-skinned enough to be a presentable house slave, but the frowns that Mrs. Turner cast in her direction made her begin to suspect that the man who put her in her mother might have been Mr. Turner himself. Even though Johnny was seldom allowed outside, the mere mention of his name caused an unparalleled terror amongst the slaves throughout the whole parish.

I'll survive this, Mariette vowed to herself as she marched up the hill to the laboratory. She could hear the chug of the steam-powered generator behind the building. It ran day and night and reminded her of a cabless locomotive with no track or cars. Heat from the engine made the air above the laboratory shimmer like a mirage. Her peg leg was sticking in the muddy road and pulling it free over and over hurt her knee and hip and made the leather straps around her thigh chafe. *I don't know how I'll survive, but I will.*

* * * *

"Come in!" Dr. Bronson called in response to her knock. "The door's not locked."

Mariette went inside. Her breath fogged in the frigid air. How could it possibly be so cold inside when it was so hot outdoors? She shivered in her thin cotton shift.

The layout of the laboratory seemed similar to the first floor of the plantation manor— Mr. Turner had hired the same architect for both. But whereas the Turners had made their entry hall into a light, airy parlor with comfortable seats, Dr. Bronson had blocked off all the windows with heavy oak bookshelves whose boards bowed under the weight of leather-bound tomes and wooden shipping boxes filled with manuscripts and correspondence. The only chair in the room sat behind a candle-lit writing desk piled with more books and papers. Deprived of sunlight and only dimly illuminated by the desk candles and gaslamps guttering in sconces, the room seemed as oppressive as a mortuary. The strange chemical stink in the air added to her goose-fleshed feeling that she'd stepped into a house of death.

"Hm." A tall, thin man of about fifty stepped from a shadow and approached her, leaning heavily on a silver-filigreed cane. He looked her up and down, disappointment clear on his gaunt, clean-shaven face. "I told the foreman to send me a boy."

Mariette set the linen basket down, mind racing to pick the words least likely to anger the scientist. "I reckon Zeke couldn't find any to send. All the men are needed for the cane harvest."

"Hm." His eyes fell on her peg. "Did you lose your leg in the fields? I'm told that a cane knife can cut a grown man nearly in two."

She shook her head. "I disobeyed Master Johnny."

"Ah. Of course. Well, I hope you intend to be more obedient here, because you'll be handling lethal substances and a failure to follow my instructions will have dire consequences."

"Yes, sir."

"I'll have you know that I do not approve of this peculiar institution of African slavery," he remarked. "The Empire should have abolished it when I was just a lad. But alas, the House of Commons rejected the Slavery Abolition Act and no one has resurrected it. I expect that it has not seemed an urgent matter ever since Charles da Vinci began producing his wondrous clockwork men."

Dr. Bronson sighed wistfully. "The best plantations have already replaced their black chattel with gleaming automatons. I keep telling my dear cousin that he should modernize his operation and replace the lot of you, but he insists that he needs your wits as well as your backs. I have my doubts as to what kind of wits are necessary to cut cane, but I do concede that the mechanical men are rather dear, and of course cannot produce more of their kind. One cannot deny the fertility of negro women."

He grimaced. "In the meantime, whites are forced to share their civilization with Africans, which inevitably leads to…miscegenation."

The simultaneously leering and disdainful look he gave her made her flush with anger, and she could not stay silent. "I was born here in Barbados. So was my mama, and *her* mama. We're Bajan. I don't know anything about Africa."

Fortunately, Dr. Bronson seemed to take her words as a statement of ignorance rather than a rebuttal to his declarations.

"I have visited that Dark Continent on several occasions, and it is a wonder." He smiled down at her. "So much gold, ivory, and diamonds! The wildlife and landscape…amazing. Truly Africa is wasted on Africans. The best thing for the place will be for European nations to colonize the whole continent and take charge of its natural resources."

"What about the Africans who live there?" She struggled to keep her tone neutral.

"Indeed! I do have a plan I intend to propose when the time is right; I admit that my reputation has become somewhat tarnished, but I fully expect that the success of my endeavors here will result in considerable acclaim. My ship shall rise on a very high tide indeed, and royals from all countries should rightly seek my advice on intellectual matters.

"But I digress. Aside from the problem of Africans, England and Europe face the problem of the underclass. Mostly people of corrupted Irish, Gyptian, and Spanish blood, you know. Those in poverty breed disease, commit crimes and foster wretchedness. Some of my colleagues think we should let the poor starve. Natural selection! But tenderhearted women and religious sorts are forever running soup kitchens and charities and the human corruption keeps spreading.

"What I propose is that we offer a low-cost, nutritionally-sound potted food to the English and European poor. The food would be spiced with silphium and asafoetida to induce infertility in the women who eat it. Thus, the poor will stay healthy enough to serve as useful workers or soldiers, but they'll stop breeding like confounded rabbits. The poor shall only exist as needed to turn the wheels of commerce. Civilization will prosper like never before!"

Mariette blinked. "That seems like a well-turned plan, sir. But what has it got to do with Africans?"

"Ah! I thought that bit was implied. Africans will serve as the meat component of the canned food. I have extensively plotted the logistics, and they're entirely economical. By the time our canneries run out of Negroes, I expect the underclass breeding problem will have been splendidly remedied."

Mariette's heart pounded and her vision was starting to go edge-dark again. In her mind, she carefully removed her peg leg and with both hands drove it straight through Bronson's loathsome chest, mud and all.

Instead, she took a deep breath, bent and picked up the linen basket, keeping her head down for fear that her eyes might show her rage. She knew she needed a few moments alone to calm herself down. Because if she was not very, very calm, she would die in this house, and Bronson would move on to the next hapless girl.

She'd spent her whole life hearing people, even other slaves, say that the world would be a better place without Negroes in it. It was common sport for the plantation owners to gather at a fish fry or around a card table to complain bitterly about the blacks who were responsible for their livelihoods. If she had a penny for every well-heeled planter who'd declared his slaves were lazy, worthless good-for-nothings who should be fed to the hogs simply because they needed to rest once in a while, she'd have been able to buy her own freedom.

Bronson's vile sentiments were common as scuttle crabs, but usually just the idle spouts of spoiled old men. The scientist clearly had ambitions and a twisted moral conviction driving him. Might his monstrous plans reach the ears of equally monstrous people who could make them real?

If there was any chance he might succeed, he had to be stopped. Even if it meant she died under Johnny's hatchet. In her mind, she saw herself creeping up to the laboratory house, blocking the doors shut with timber, and dousing it with lamp oil. It was easy and terrible to imagine Bronson screaming as he burned inside with all his notes.

But perhaps there was a better way that didn't end in fire? She wouldn't know until she found out what he was trying to do. Mr. Turner had surely not brought Bronson here to refine his plans to turn Africans into potted meat. The laboratory work must have something to do with curing Johnny's madness…or anyhow the doctor had convinced Mr. Turner that it did.

"Would you like me to change your bedclothes, sir?"

"Certainly, but be quick about it; I'll need you in the lab shortly."

* * * *

Mariette followed Bronson into a short hallway that was even colder than the foyer study, and she could more clearly hear the chug of the steam engine along with the electrical hum of some other kind of apparatus. Twin gaslights brightly illuminated the hall, which only had room for a narrow table along one wall and a rail of wooden coat hooks along the other. A couple of long, padded canvas coats and brass goggles hung from the rack.

"Remove anything you might have in your pockets and leave it on the table." Bronson frowned at her peg leg. "Is that secured with iron or steel nails?"

She shook her head. "It has bronze buckles and such, but the rest is leather and wood."

"Any iron or steel at all?"

"No sir."

"Good. Do you know letters and numbers?"

"Only a little." Mariette's heart beat fast at the lie. Unlike most of the slaves on the plantation, she had learned to read quite well, but her instincts were telling her that she should keep her knowledge close to her bosom. Bronson needed to underestimate her.

As a house slave, Mariette was expected to follow simple directions and recipes and to take messages from visitors. And so she'd been taught to read and write along with Mr. Turner's youngest children. Her lessons ended once she knew practical words like "fish" and "sugar" and "cup".

But while Mariette was still recovering from her amputation, Mr. Turner's mother Helen—possibly her own grandmother, she now realized—started to go blind. Helen loved penny dreadfuls shipped in from England and read them by the boxload until her vision began to fail. None of Mr. Turner's legitimate children had the time for (or interest in) reading to their granny. And so the elder Mrs. Turner enlisted Mariette to read her stories and London newspapers aloud to her. It was hard, at first, but the old lady was eager enough for entertainment and company that she patiently gave Mariette the proper pronunciations once she spelled out unfamiliar words.

"You best not let on to anyone how well you can read," Mrs. Turner said one day when Mariette brought in her afternoon tea. "Folks don't trust slaves with too-sharp minds. Can't say I blame them, but I reckon you're one of the good ones, so it can be our little secret."

The old lady's words were a cozy lambswool shawl draped over a cane knife: *Displease me, and I'll destroy you.*

But Mariette was adept at keeping her perhaps-grandmother happy. The girl's starving mind absorbed the informal tutoring, and soon she was sneaking into the library at night and reading more difficult books, puzzling them out by candlelight with the aid of the huge cloth-bound copy of Johnson's *Dictionary* that roosted on the bottom shelf. During the day, she took great care to dust the library thoroughly so that no one would see the tracks of books being pulled from shelves.

She read the entire works of Shakespeare, and but kept returning to his play *The Tempest*. It was mostly because of the magic-filled story, which she could easily picture happening there on Barbados. But it was also because of Caliban and Miranda. She hated him for trying to rape her, but at the same time she thought that he was right to resent her father Prospero, who pretended he'd done Caliban a favor by enslaving him. And Miranda had no freedom at all, even though she got her handsome prince. The play's happy ending didn't fully satisfy her mind, and she felt compelled to re-read it, as if the words would rearrange themselves and some other ending might emerge.

If there had been any books on Africa, she'd have surely read and re-read them, too, but the subject was of no interest to the Turners.

"I can read some recipes and such," she told Bronson. The other house slaves knew she could read that much, and admitting it meant he'd be less likely to catch her lie.

"Hm," He seemed disappointed. "I suppose I am the victim of wishful thinking, as ever. The African mind is not suited to higher thought processes, but I do miss having helpers who can read things for themselves."

This time, the peg leg she wielded in her mind went straight through his eye and out the back of his skull.

Instead, she said, "I will do my best despite my mental deficiencies, sir."

At that, his eyes narrowed a bit and his eyebrows went up, but she kept her face carefully neutral and his moment of suspicion that she was being sarcastic apparently passed. He took one of the padded canvas coats and one set of the brass goggles from the rack and handed them to her.

"Put these on. There are gloves in the pockets of the coat; put them on, too. Button it up to your neck; you'll want the protection from the cold."

She did as he asked. The gloves she found were made of a thinner waxed canvas and had leather palms and fingertips like Mrs. Turner's gardening gloves. Everything was several sizes too big for her, but she was able to cinch the strap on the goggles down over her head scarf so that the heavy leaded glass lenses stayed in place over her eyes.

Bronson reached for the bronze knob of the door leading into what had to be the main laboratory and paused, giving her a sharp look. "You are about to embark on a most noble endeavor. It's entirely possible—and, if you fail to obey me, highly likely—that you shall lose your life in this room. But know that you are doing it for the greater good of mankind."

Despite the disdain he seemed to have for her, there was a showman's gleam in his eye. He craved an audience, Mariette realized. And if she were careful in her questions, she could use his eagerness to good advantage.

"What will we be doing, sir? Is it something to help Johnny Turner?"

"He will be helped, yes, but my research will do far more."

Bronson opened the door into the laboratory. There was a strange burnt smell like the air after lightning struck a tree. The first thing Mariette saw was a pair of huge round glass tanks conjoined by a glass box with leather-covered portholes. Each of the round tanks was seamed with riveted brass strips and had enormous gleaming coils of copper wire at the top and bottom.

In the tank to her left, a strange, pulsing mass floated mid-air between the coils. It writhed bonelessly like a living thing. One moment it seemed black as tar, the next red as the setting sun, the next white as the moon. Even though it gave off no strong light, looking directly at it made her eyes ache, and she felt the exposed skin on her face grow warm as if she were standing beneath the noonday sun despite the cold of the room.

"What is that?" Mariette squinted away from the tanks and finally noticed the wall of brass instrument panels and racks of wooden tongs and blown glass bubbles. Thick rubber-coated cables ran from the copper coils to sockets in the base of the panels.

"Achronic aether," Bronson replied proudly. His breath fogged away from him as if he were not a man but a dragon exhaling smoke. "Others have postulated its existence; I am the first to distill it and contain it. And soon, I shall be the only man able to control it."

"W-what does it do?" Her teeth were starting to chatter, whether from fear or physical chill she couldn't tell.

"At the moment, it strips heat from air, life from flesh, and sanity from minds," he replied. "But once it is properly tamed, it shall make me master of both time and space."

She stared at the blob again despite her discomfort, and she felt the hairs rise on the back of her neck beneath her stiff canvas collar. "How?"

"You're beholding a fundamental solvent of the universe. We think of time and distances as fixed, linear. Trinidad is 60 leagues away; even if you took to the skies in a dirigible, you still have to travel the distance. Christmas is seven months away, and the faithful must suffer through every day between now and then. But with a stabilized crystal of achronic aether, a man of intelligence can escape the mundane bonds of time and distance and go when and where he wishes."

Mariette blinked, thinking of Scrooge and his glimpse of the future in Charles Dickens' *A Christmas Carol*. "He could go where and when…and change his fate?"

"Of course!" Bronson's laugh was equal parts delight and scorn. "There's no profit in merely being an observer! The possessor of the crystal could go to the future to discover wonders not yet invented…or go into the past and change his own starting fortunes entirely. The possibilities are limitless! But, as per my agreement with your owner, my first proof-of-concept will be to go back in time to convince Johnny Turner to stay here in Barbados instead of joining the British Navy."

Her stomach buzzed as if she, too, had been hooked up to the electrical current from the great steam engine laboring outside. The achronic aether pulsed emerald inside its magnetic glass cage. No science could prove it, but she was certain it was eyelessly observing her.

"How many assistants have you had, sir?"

"Oh, seventy or eighty…I've rather lost count." He paused. "Ours is a world of hundreds of millions of people. One might believe that an individual can have no possible consequence in the swarming sea of humanity, but history has proved otherwise over and over. Imagine that the great Leonardo da Vinci had left no heirs…would the world now have clockwork men and flying machines? He mattered; and soon, I shall matter even more."

* * * *

Day after day, Mariette took the painful hike up the hill to the laboratory, where she did exactly what Bronson told her to do. It was an endless, nerve-wracking repetition of getting a pair of wooden tongs and a round flask, using the glove box to coax a bit of the aether from the first chamber into the glass, and then quickly transferring the aether-laden flask into the second chamber. Once she'd gotten it into that second chamber, she had to hold it perfectly still as Bronson worked his control panel to increase the magnetic fields to try to crush the aether into a crystalline configuration.

If the magnetic field ever failed, the aether would eat through the side of the glass and then through the tongs, and then the substance would behave as if she had dropped it. And if she ever dropped it, one of two immediately fatal things were likely to occur. The aether might explode into a fine black mist that would latch onto the nearest source of heat and moisture: her. And it would freeze her entire body solid before it dissipated back into the cracks of the universe. The second thing was that the aether might stay intact, but would ring like the very bell of doom, vibrating at a frequency guaranteed to drive most people insane if they were close by, and perhaps turn their brains to soup if they were quite near. Bronson had designed the room so that his seat at the instrument panel was a safe distance away.

Mariette did not drop the glass. Every day, she silently prayed to the Christian God and the forbidden Obeah spirits alike that Bronson would keep the magnetic field working. And when he wasn't looking, she strained her eyes to glimpse his notes and try to figure out what he intended to do once he had his crystal. But she gained no useful clues from his scribbles and equations.

At the end of each session, Mariette's shoulders, hands, leg and eyes ached, and her face was as dark as if she'd worked the entire time in the fields. She fell into an exhausted slumber and dreamed of strange worlds far beyond the Earth. She got Sunday afternoons off, as did all of Mr. Turner's slaves after they'd attended church and dutifully listened to the white preacher's sermons, but she found it harder and harder to make small talk with the others. Just as each day she and Bronson drew minutely closer to getting the aether to conform, each day she felt as though her mind was being forced open and taken away into a dimension of probability and causality. Even the Crop Over celebration, which she'd looked forward to every year since she was a small child, couldn't bring her drifting mind back to shore.

But one day in November, Mariette was grimly clutching the tongs as she tried to keep the flask-bound aether steady in the second chamber. Bronson was trying the 316th new magnetic bombardment pattern he'd designed since Zeke ordered her to the laboratory; she had counted them all. Suddenly the aether crackled like hot molasses candy dropping into ice water. In a blink it had collapsed into a perfect, iridescent tetragon that rang like a silver bell.

And in that moment, she nearly dropped it in surprise and wonder, but she held fast at the last minute.

"Sir, sir, come quick!" Mariette had no faith that the aether would be stable and hold its shape for more than a few seconds.

She heard the clatter of Bronson knocking over the tongs rack in his haste to join her.

"Bring it forth!" he demanded.

"But it—"

"Bring it forth!"

Mariette took a deep breath and pulled the flask out of the chamber through the glove box porthole. Once released from the magnetic field, the bean-sized crystal clinked to the bottom of the glass. For one terrible moment, she was certain it was about to explode or eat through the flask, but it glittered perfect and still. Stable.

"Hold it up to the light!" Bronson wore the ecstatic expression of an atheist who had finally found God.

She carried the flask over to a nearby lamp so that Bronson could examine it more closely. Her mind churned. She'd spent so much time in the laboratory that she wanted very badly to see if the crystal worked as Bronson predicted…but she could not forget the terrible fates he wished on people like her. And he'd never revealed how it was that he intended to actually use the crystal. Even his notes had shed no light on that part of his plan. Should she wait and see? Should she fling the crystal against the wall to destroy it and probably herself and Bronson, too?

To her profound surprise, Bronson snatched the flask out of the tongs with his bare hands.

Bronson's eye grew wide with wonder, as if he saw something miraculous in the far distance. "It's…"

But then his body jerked as if he'd been struck and his eyes went dull, unresponsive. His knees buckled and the flask slipped from his lifeless fingers.

Mariette lunged forward to catch the flask in her gloved hands before it could shatter on the hard wooden floor.

The moment the glass-clad crystal settled in the palm of her gloved hand, the laboratory seemed to fall away and she felt as though she were floating in the vast, cold darkness amongst the stars.

"I have been summoned." The voice was all around her. "What do you wish? Choose."

"Who are you?" she whispered, terrified.

"Ylem."

Suddenly, the vast wave of all the possibilities in the entire universe crashed down around her. She could go to any time, any world, any dimension, anywhere. The capacity of her mind expanded as fast as light, but it could not keep up with the infinity of possibility in the universe.

"Choose," Ylem demanded. "I have been summoned, and you must choose."

The impossibility of choice in the face of infinity threatened to burn her mind down like a blade of grass caught in a supernova.

But nonetheless, she chose: "I don't want to be a slave. I don't want to have been a slave. I don't want *any* human being to have suffered as we have."

"You have chosen. Now, make it so."

The lines of history and probability and causality opened before her mind like a vast treasure map, and she raced backward through the ages, an Angel of Death for some, a guardian ghost to others. To kill, she had to but brush her spectral hand through a ribcage to stop a heart. To save a dying infant, she had to but picture healthy lungs or a full belly and it was so. But the more greed and evil she erased, the more there seemed to be. Slavery was intertwined with war and conquest so deeply that it was impossible to separate the two. And the wars seemed to go back forever and ever.

After what seemed like an aeon of saving and slaying, she found herself upon a sun-bleached veldt. A family of dark, slender, slightly-built apes clung to each other, keening softly as a gang of tall, burly apes from a different tribe surrounded them, hooting in victory and brandishing sharpened sticks.

She saw into the minds of the big apes. They would slay all the small males and roast them over the fire they had recently learned to capture from lightning strikes. But they might leave some of the small females alive as breeding slaves. These big apes delighted in killing and taking territory, reveled in the misery of the others they drove before them.

And she saw the minds of the small ones. They, too, had learned to use fire to harden clay for pots and beads and to boil the grains they foraged. The small ones delighted in making love and singing and crafting and only killed when they could find no plants or grubs to eat.

Mariette made her choice.

"It is accomplished," Ylem said when she stopped the heart of the last big ape.

For a moment, Mariette found herself back in the lab, staring down at the crystal in the flask in her gloved hands as Bronson lay dead at her feet.

And then the crystal evaporated and the laboratory melted away.

Mariette—no, her name was Kmbana of the Green—stood on the deck of a ship floating above the clouds, staring down into empty hands. Hands that were brown and quite narrow and which bore short red fur. Completely familiar and yet utterly alien.

"Are you all right?" trilled her sister Nmbena in a language so far from English that she could not compare the two, but she knew it just as well.

Kmbana looked up at her sister's earnest amber eyes and excitable whiskers and made herself smile. "Yes. I'm fine. Just daydreaming."

Her mind now held two completely different memories: her life as the slave Mariette, and her new life as Kmbana, and her brain reeled trying to reconcile it all.

"Do you like the new leg?" her sister asked.

"Oh yes," Kmbana replied reflexively as she suddenly remembered that here, in this new *now*, she'd lost her leg falling over the edge of an airship when she was just a child. "It's lovely."

And it *was* lovely, she realized. It was a gorgeous work of wood and brass made to match her flesh leg, and inside it had clever tiny motors and clockworks to allow her to move the metal foot like a real one.

"It's amazing," Kmbana added.

"Do you think you would like to take a walk along the seashore? The shipmothers are talking about stopping at the island below us."

Her sister pointed over the railing at a teardrop-shaped island, and Kmbana gave a start when she recognized it from the shape she'd once seen on maps: Barbados! She breathed in the smells of rich soil and seaweed. But here it was the tip of a nameless archipelago. She tried to make out the rise where the plantation would have been, but it was all forest.

She wanted to laugh with joy at the wonders of this peaceful new world, but she also wanted to weep for the good she'd inadvertently erased along with the bad. She and her sister and the other millions of souls upon the planet were people, certainly, but none human as she understood humanity. There had never been a British Navy, nor a Johnny Turner to be twisted by it. But there also had never been a Dickens, nor a da Vinci, nor a Shakespeare. There had been others just as brilliant—the Great Mothers they learned about in school—and people had accomplished immortal works of art and invention in the absence of war. But they were not the same.

It made her profoundly sad to know that she would never read *The Tempest* again.

Apparently her expression clouded, because her sister added, "I think we might be the first to visit this island. We might get to name things we find! Wouldn't you like that?"

Kmbana smiled. "Yes, I'd like that."

Dolmen of The Moon
by Deuce Richardson

It looms, as I stand in the shadows' length,
Amazed before a cyclopean Door.
Immense it rises there, in sullen strength.
Strength that many a tempest bore.

On the threshold, with sudden pause,
I hear a ghostly echo of titanic claws.
My soul, whose fears I cannot quell
Bids me kneel down and murmur low
Incantations of warding, as I know
Therein ancient, dark secrets dwell.

~ Fr. Wm. von Junzt ~

Ancient Astronauts

by Cynthia Ward

We've been observing your Earth
And one night we'll make
A contact with you
- Klaatu, "Calling Occupants of Interplanetary Craft"

Penobscot County, Maine, October 31, 1979

As the Carpenters' cover of "Calling Occupants of Interplanetary Craft" started playing, Mike pointed at the transistor radio in the basket on Joanna's handlebar.

"What do you think of the book?"

She realized he was pointing at the battered paperback leaning against the radio.

"Just started it," she said. "I've seen the movie based on *Chariots of the Gods?*, though. It's awesome."

Mike smiled. "Bet you weren't seven years old when you saw it. How much can you remember?"

"How could I forget alien astronauts?" Joanna said. "They were worshipped as gods. They built landing fields in South America, the ancient pyramids—all sorts of stuff!"

Mike's smile faded. "Did they build Stonehenge?"

"I don't remember the movie mentioning that." Joanna frowned in concentration. "I think the Celts built it."

Mike looked intently up the road, like there was traffic to watch for, even though their friend Bradley's house was on a dead-end street outside the town limits of Norumbega.

Joanna said, "Indians built the standing stones at Indian Point and Chesuncook, didn't they?"

"Those were built by nothing human," Mike said, still looking straight ahead.

"That's why I want to read the book," Joanna said. "The movie missed some stuff. It didn't mention the Old Ones or Cthulhu or the shoggoths. You hardly ever see Maine in books, unless they're Stephen King books. But the Old Ones had outposts right here in Maine, at Chesuncook and just north of the Indian Point Reservation!"

Mike lived on the reservation with all the other Penobscots, so he should know this stuff, but he kept staring forwards.

Joanna faced forwards as they continued up the road. They both had licenses, but they didn't have cars. Not many kids did.

The Atlanta Rhythm Section's "So Into You" came on the radio. Joanna stole a look at Mike. He was looking at a V of migrating Canada geese and never noticed.

She risked a longer look. Mike was tall and bony and his black hair was as short as Davy's blond hair. He had glasses and a couple of pimples, but so did she. He was as smart as his older brother but not as athletic. His brother'd gotten a football scholarship at the University of Maine at Orono, and he had broad shoulders and a square, handsome face. But Joanna thought Mike was just as good-looking. Plus, Mike liked science fiction books and *Star Wars*. Not many people did.

As the song went into the instrumental part, Joanna said, "You've never mentioned the Old Ones, Mike. Did you know the Penobscots used to worship them?"

Mike looked at her with a stony expression and touched the little silver crucifix showing at the V of his button-down shirt. "We worshipped the Creator before the fathers told us of Christ. Only a few degenerates ever worshipped devils."

"Oh," Joanna said. "I didn't know."

"It's okay." Mike faced forwards. "What's Bradley doing?"

Joanna looked up the street. There were woods on both sides, but they didn't come all the way to the hot top here, and the intervening property had a long field with a few black and white cows behind an electric fence. She and Mike could see Bradley's parents' property clearly, and old Harold Waite's property on the other side.

Joanna spoke in a puzzled tone. "It looks like Bradley's walking acrosst his dooryard to Mr. Waite's field."

The song faded and the deejay started talking. "It's Halloween, when 'devil worshippers' used to make sacrifices to 'Elder Things from outer space' at the standing stones near Chesuncook and Norumbega. But—" the male voice gave a hollow laugh as "The Monster Mash" began to play "—no one's ever seen the devils—or the worshippers. I think they're partying with Boris Karloff's ghost, myself."

"The Dyer expedition saw some dead Old Ones, a long time ago in Antarctica," Joanna said. "But nobody's ever managed to get back to—what on earth? Bradley is going on Mr. Waite's property."

"You know what else is weird?" Mike said. "Mr. Waite is sitting in the middle of the seat of his pickup. And Mr. Levesque is sitting next to the passenger door."

"Bradley doesn't like Mr. Waite," Joanna muttered. "Actually, no one likes Mr. Waite. Or Mr. Levesque, either."

"And vice-versa," Mike said.

Joanna hadn't realized he'd know this, living on the reservation.

He frowned. "Bradley's getting behind the wheel of Mr. Waite's old Ford."

Joanna noticed she and Mike had stopped their bicycles.

A chill gust cut through her flannel Bean shirt. Dry leaves swirled around them. She smelled a trace of smoke from some distant woodstove or fireplace.

She shut off the radio.

Bradley started Mr. Waite's car and looked around.

Joanna shivered. "Bradley's face looks weird."

"You're right." Mike spoke softly, like Bradley could hear them, and Joanna realized she'd been whispering. "Bradley's frowning just like Mr. Waite."

Howard Waite was always scowling and suspicious-looking, when you saw him. He got shot in the leg in a hunting accident, a long time ago, and could barely walk. He lived alone in an old farmhouse he'd inherited from a distant relative long before Joanna was born, and was practically a recluse. That was okay, though, because you didn't really like to see him. He was scary-looking, with an angry, shriveled old face that was so pop-eyed, it looked almost like a fish's. She'd overheard Mrs. Beal, who was over a hundred years old, saying "That nasty ol' bastid Harold Waite come to Maine from Innsmouth. There's something not quite human in the blood of Innsmouth people."

Her parents wouldn't tell her what it was.

They didn't need to, though.

She knew his ancestors were ancient astronauts.

Bradley noticed her and Mike standing on the side of the street, just far enough from the edge to avoid the poison ivy.

After glaring at them for several seconds, Bradley smiled and waved.

Joanna and Mike waved back.

Their smiles were as fake as Bradley's.

She said, "Bradley's smile looks like—like Mr. Waite's would, if he ever smiled."

Bradley started his neighbor's truck.

"Where's Bradley going?" Mike muttered. "He invited us over so he could teach us that game his cousin in Portland taught him—what's it called?"

"Dragons and Dungeons, I think," Joanna replied. "Maybe Mr. Waite got sick and Bradley's taking him to the doc—Jeezum Crow. Bradley's not going to the doctor. He's driving up Mr. Waite's driveway and right acrosst his field."

"Mr. Waite hardly goes anywheres," Mike said, "and he doesn't go anywheres with anyone else."

Joanna whispered, "You ever hear that old story—that Mr. Waite can put his mind in other people's heads?"

"He's from Massachusetts, what else do you expect?" Mike smiled to show he was joking, but he didn't look like he thought it was funny. He looked kind of sick.

Following the dirt road, Bradley drove the old man's pickup into the woods.

"You know where that road goes?" Mike asked Joanna.

"I don't know any more than you do," she replied.

"I know the direction he's headed," Mike said.

"North." Joanna shivered. "Towards the standing stones beyond Indian Point."

Without another word, Mike and Joanna resumed bicycling.

* * * *

Some said the hole in the woods north of Indian Point was bottomless. Others said it led to the hollow earth, where the Old Ones and shoggoths had slept since abandoning the earth's surface, eons ago. The shoggoths and their creators were supposed to be immortal and nearly indestructible. Sometimes they came up the hole, Mrs. Beal said, but nobody reliable had ever reported seeing a shoggoth or Old One anywheres north of the Merrimack River.

The hole wasn't too far from the west bank of the Penobscot. If the dirt road Mike and Joanna had followed for miles through the woods went to the river, or even the hole, they didn't know. They might not find out, either. Through the denuded maples, they could see someone at a bend in the road, standing guard with a shotgun in his hands.

They kept glancing back, but he didn't notice as they retreated up the road.

They were lucky it hadn't rained lately, Joanna thought. The fallen leaves covering the rutted road were damp underneath, so their bicycles had slipped and almost fallen several times. But at least they weren't riding through mud. If they had been, they probably never would've gotten here.

Would that be so bad? whispered a little voice in her head.

They stopped walking on the far side of a hill.

Mike looked at Joanna and spoke so softly, she had to read his lips.

"Rocky Hill overlooks the hole and the circle of standing stones."

Joanna looked at the hill. Its slopes were bare granite, covered with rocks and boulders. The hill wasn't very high, but it was broad, and it was steep on every side. It was hard to understand why the rocks hadn't all rolled off long ago.

She swallowed.

"It won't be easy to climb."

"It's okay," Mike murmured. "We don't have to climb it."

She flushed, realizing he'd understood why she wouldn't climb it, the one time she and Mike and Bradley had come to see the hole and standing stones.

Did Bradley realize it, too? Or did Mike tell him she was afraid of heights? The idea of them both knowing deepened her mortification.

She took a shuddering breath.

"We have to climb it," she said. "If we try to sneak through the trees, we might be heard by the guy with the gun."

Climbing the hill wasn't easy.

To distract herself, Joanna remembered the time they'd bicycled to the hole with Bradley, even though Bradley didn't like hiking or bicycling all that much. But it was the summer before their sophomore year. Nobody had a driver's license.

Joanna had made herself glance in the hole. There were stairs carved right in the granite of the round, almost tube-like sides. The stairs went down past where the sun could reach, though it was the middle of the day.

She looked around the clearing. The standing stones were spray-painted with graffiti. A lot of McDonalds wrappers and empty bottles and cigarette butts and roaches were scattered around. Sometimes kids came here at night—the place wasn't too far off the Old Millinocket Road—to party or have sex.

Joanna had never done any of those things, here or anywheres else. She supposed Mike and Bradley hadn't, either. They weren't in the party crowd at school, and she didn't have a boyfriend, and Mike and Bradley didn't have girlfriends.

Bradley smiled at Mike. "You ought to bring Molly Sockbeson here!"

Molly Sockbeson was a Penobscot girl who'd been in some of their freshman college-track classes at Norumbega High. Joanna hadn't thought Mike had noticed her. But Bradley's remark made Mike's face darken.

"Why don't *you* bring somebody?" Mike asked Bradley.

Bradley waved a hand. "I'm waiting to meet the right girl." He laughed. "Did you forget I'm born again? Even if I had a girlfriend, we'd wait until we got married."

Then he turned red, realizing he'd implied a good Catholic girl like Molly would have premarital sex.

Then Joanna realized Bradley wasn't thinking that, or not *only* thinking that, because he looked at her and said, "I don't mean we came here to do that with you—we're not—I mean—"

He stopped talking with his mouth open.

Mike smiled at Joanna. "He means, you're one of the guys."

The ultimate compliment, she'd thought, and the ultimate insult.

She and Mike were getting close to the top of the hill.

She turned her memory to the time she overheard Mrs. Beal saying some white men had gone down the stairs to see what was in the "bottom-less hole," back when the town of Norumbega was founded, centuries ago. None of those men had ever returned. Later, the town had laid a gate made of thick, crisscrossed iron bars acrosst the hole and sunk big iron spikes in the granite to hold the gate in place. The bars and hinges were old and rusty, but nobody could break them. But every few years, a guy or couple went missing, and when the Penobscot County Sheriff's Office investi-gated the area, they usually found the massive padlock broken off and the gate open. The deputies never found the missing people, or even, Mrs. Beal claimed, went in the hole.

Joanna and Mike reached the top of the hill. It was covered with tall white pines and fallen pine needles. The sun was sinking almost directly behind them, but the trees kept them in shadow as they crossed the summit and knelt at the edge.

Looking down from the crest, Joanna felt sick from the height. She couldn't bear to look down the hole. But she could see the gate was open. The hole and several of the standing stones were still in sunlight.

They were alone on the hill, but they weren't alone.

There were about a dozen white people within the ring of standing stones. Most of them stood facing the hole from the south side. These people were in shadow, but Joanna could tell they were all adults and all wearing gray robes. It was kind of tricky to judge from above, but they were mostly old and mostly men. She didn't recognize anybody until one of the three men holding shotguns looked around. He'd been guarding the road earlier.

On the western side of the hole, Mr. Waite—or his body—lay on a flat, rectangular stone. Joanna shivered. She couldn't help thinking of the stone table Aslan was killed on, in *The Lion, the Witch and the Wardrobe*.

The aged body was tied to the altar-stone with thick ropes. It writhed like its occupant was trying to escape and made sounds against its gag. The eyes were wide, with an expression like the one Bradley got the time he was almost hit by a car.

Clad in gray robes, Bradley's body and Mr. Levesque stood on the north side of the hole. Mr. Levesque was so close to the altar, he was half in shadow. In the sunlight, Bradley's body faced the group with an open book on his left palm and a knife in his right fist, though Bradley was left-handed. He spoke to the crowd with the expressions and intonations and Massachusetts accent of Harold Waite.

"—and I remind you," said the voice, "the mind is independent of the body, and need never perish. Once, it could transfer from body to body forever, by means of the secret lost with my uncle, Ephraim Waite. But I have been communing with the dweller below. And tonight, I promise you:

"The Old One shall accept our sacrifice, and teach us another way to transfer our minds from body to body, and thereby live forever!"

"You were right, Joanna," Mike murmured. "Mr. Waite can do soul transfers. And he wants to kill Bradley in his own body, so his soul can stay in Bradley's body and avoid God's judgment."

Joanna didn't know if there was a God or not, never mind a judgment, but the question seemed irrelevant at the moment.

She whispered, "How in Hell do we stop them from killing Bradley?"

As she fell silent, a bizarre creature flew from the hole. It had a barrel-shaped body, with one starfish-shaped appendage at the top and another at the bottom. The creature's sides sprouted five leathery wings longer than the six-foot barrel.

Recognizing the creature from descriptions she'd read, Joanna inhaled in awe.

"An ancient astronaut!" she whispered.

"A devil," Mike muttered.

The Old One rose higher than the hill. Mike and Joanna kept motionless as the sunlit creature started circling above the circle of standing stones. The top slabs of the still-standing pairs were about ten feet below the hilltop.

Some of the five eyes and five cilia in the Old One's starfish-like head must have detected the seventeen-year-old juniors, Joanna Saltonstall and Mike Francis, in the shadow of the pines, for the Old One started winging towards them.

"O great and wise Elder God," cried Bradley in Harold Waite's accent, "what are you doing?"

Breaking his crucifix off its fine chain, Mike leaped into the air.

At impact, he wrapped his arms and legs around the tapering top of the barrel-body and hung on, like a movie stunt-man jumping on a bronco's neck from the front. Under their combined weights, the Old One dipped towards the granite cross-piece on the pair of stones standing directly below. Joanna realized Mike was pressing his crucifix against the Old One's leathery stump of a neck.

Mike shouted, "The power of Christ compels you:

"Return to Hell!"

The Old One stopped its fall by catching itself on its wings. It raised tentacles from where they'd rested, unnoticed, against its barrel-body. It reached for Mike, clearly intending to pull him off and throw him to his death.

Joanna jumped.

She landed so far back on the barrel, she missed Mike's arms and legs and banged into a wing.

Their combined weights sent the Old One plummeting out of the air.

She'd thought she'd been afraid before.

She'd never been afraid, compared to this.

She struck the nearest tentacle with the stone she'd grabbed as she leaped.

The Old One slammed into the slab.

The impact sent the trio of massive stones tumbling, to strike more of the stones standing in the ancient circle.

As the stones toppled, the people below screamed and the shotguns went off.

The Old One struggled to rise on its five wings.

The two that had been beneath its body on impact hung uselessly.

Its trajectory altered by the broken wings, the Old One fell towards the hole.

As Joanna jerked her head up from the glimpse of its depths, Mike cried, "Jump!"

Leaping on the Old One had been an almost lateral jump.

She couldn't jump down.

She'd fall down the hole—the bottomless hole—

She jumped.

* * * *

"Jeezum Crow," Joanna murmured. "Looks like almost everyone fell in the hole except us and Brad—Bradley's body."

"God's judgment," Mike said. "The standing stones have killed Mr. Waite and Mr. Levesque, and blocked the rest of the devil-worshippers in the hole. May God keep the Old Ones and their worshippers and shoggoths trapped in Hell forevermore."

Joanna suspected not every worshipper had been trapped. She'd glimpsed people on the other side of the hole running away as the stones fell. But the bodies of Mr. Waite and Mr. Levesque lay under a slab, and she felt no pulses in their exposed wrists. As for any survivors, they wouldn't reveal what had happened, even if they'd recognized her or Mike. Nobody'd want to admit to human sacrifice or worship of the Old Ones.

She'd hit the ground so hard, she supposed she'd been knocked out.

The sun wasn't much lower, though, judging by the light. Her hip hurt, but not as much as her left shoulder and arm. She'd never felt anything that bad. She resumed cradling her left arm and didn't look at the weird bend in the middle of the forearm.

"Bradley!" she whispered. "Is he okay? Is he—Bradley?"

Bradley's body had escaped the falling stones, but whoever was inside the body was unconscious. From shock or fear, maybe. Joanna couldn't see any damage.

Mike was conscious, but worse off. His left leg was bent in the middle of the calf. His black pants had ripped open and both legs were scraped and bleeding from ankle to knee. He'd landed some distance from Bradley's body, but he could reach the toe of one of Bradley's sneakers with a fingertip. He tapped on the sneaker and spoke.

"Bradley?"

Well, Joanna thought, at least nobody got shot.

She went to the brook trickling through the woods a few yards away and cupped water in her good hand. The water was so cold, you'd think she'd broken through winter ice to get it. She came back and dribbled water on Bradley's face.

"Bradley?" she said.

"Bradley Greenwood!" Mike said. "Wake up."

Bradley's eyes opened, blue as ever, but confused.

A pit opened in Joanna's stomach.

Bradley's eyes focused on her face, then Mike's.

"It was terrible," whispered Bradley's voice. "Being trapped in that old body with all its aches and pains, and anyways it felt *wrong*. It wasn't *mine*. I knew even before I opened my eyes.

"And Mr. Waite was sitting on one side of me, in *my* body. And Mr. Levesque was on the other side, telling me he'd break every bone in my new body if I didn't keep still. Then I realized Mr. Waite was going to kill me and live in my body, and everybody would think he was me, and no one would ever know, and I don't know what he would've done to *you guys*, or *my family, or*—"

"It's over," Joanna said softly. "Mr. Waite and Mr. Levesque are dead, and a bunch of standing stones have fallen on the hole."

"The devils are never getting out again," Mike said.

Bradley closed his eyes with an expression of relief.

When he looked at them again, he said, "Oh my gosh, you're hurt!"

"Don't worry," Mike said. "You can drive us and our bicycles out of here in Mr. Waite's pickup."

"That's not enough to repay you for saving me from—"

"All right," Mike said. "You can also make up an explanation of what happened to us that doesn't land us in jail or the Bangor Mental Health Institute."

"That's not enough, either," Bradley protestd.

"It's all you're going to get," Joanna told him.

"Well," Bradley said, with a glance at Mike, "I can tell Molly Sockbeson what hap—"

"No you won't," Mike said. He turned to Joanna with a grin. "He's Bradley, all right."

"He is," Joanna said.

She looked away from Mike.

"Okay, okay," Bradley said. "Nobody will ever know. Even Molly."

"Deal," said Mike.

All the way home in the jouncing pickup, "So Into You" went around and around in Joanna's head, repeating its lyrics of a relationship that never ended, because it never started.

Lovecraftian Limerick
by Andrew J. Wilson

There once were some fungi from Yuggoth
Who battled the protean shoggoth,
    And those creatures of myth
    Called the Great Race of Yith,
Before falling foul of Yog-Sothoth.

The Thing in the Pond
by John R. Fultz

They say Old Man Carter started digging the pond back in 1931. His wife and two little boys had died from tuberculosis. Folks said he'd lost his mind. He never even shed a tear at the funeral, but as soon as his family was laid to rest he went on home and started digging. Most folks thought he was digging a well at first. Others claimed he was digging the pond that his poor wife had always wanted. I remember my granddaddy's take on it:

"Jeb Carter is plum crazy."

Some men deal with grief in unexpected ways. Old Man Carter turned his grief into a sadness that would mar the earth itself. He dug, and he dug, and he dug. Folks brought him sandwiches from the General Store and farmers' wives brought him chicken dinners. After a week the hole was forty feet deep, and they lowered his meals into the hole with a bucket-and-rope. Carter had rigged up a pulley system to haul up buckets of dislocated earth all day long, and a few local boys helped moved the dirt piles aside to make room for more. Everybody figured he'd give it up eventually.

Carter stayed in that damp hole, sleeping only when he'd exhausted himself, then getting right back up and digging again. All day every day—dig, dig, dig. He sent up the loose dirt in five-gallon buckets one at a time. People even came from other counties to stand at the top of the hole and watch Jeb Carter digging his way to nowhere.

"He's bound to hit China someday if'n he don't quit," some said.

"Shee-it, he'll die before he digs that far," said others.

"I read a book says they's fires deep in the earth," said a boy. "Fire and magma. He keeps on digging he'll open up Hell itself. Burn 'im alive."

"He's lost his mind," they all agreed, but nobody could blame him.

After all, he'd lost everything else.

So after a while most folks forgot all about Carter and his hole. That is until the hole filled up with water that spewed out to drown the whole pasture overnight. Nobody saw Carter come out of that hole, and the county men said he'd struck some underground reservoir or river that had proceeded to drown him. In less than a day there was no more sign of the crazy old man or his hole. There was just a big pond of deep green water, sparkling in the sunlight.

Nobody went near the Carter place for months. Down at the barber shop folks would mention Old Carter and imagine his bones lying at the bottom of the pond, or maybe stuck deep down in the hole that had birthed it. At night the pond was a black mirror reflecting the stars, and the smell of the deep earth hung in the air about it.

Wild things don't fear what men fear, so it wasn't long before the pond was lousy with fat, burping frogs. A forest of tall reeds grew about its edges. A few years later, a group of young boys snuck out to the Carter pond to hunt bullfrogs. Seven boys went down there after midnight, but only six came home. I was one of those boys, so I can tell you what happened.

Johnny Haxton, always the wildest of our bunch, decided to go for a moonlight swim. The other boys stalked the reed forest, stabbing their three-pointed gigs into every frog they could find. Johnny yelled at us to jump in. "The water's fine, boys!" he said. I remember him doing the backstroke, and I almost took off my muddy shirt and joined him.

Then I heard a gulping sound and Johnny was gone. In the center of the pond a ring of quiet ripples marked the place where he had been. I dropped an impaled frog into the burlap sack I was carrying and watched the ripples, waiting for Johnny to come back up. After about thirty seconds I started calling his name. I saw his hand come up once, the water splashing, and something dark as a shadow emerged for a half-second. Johnny's hand went back under, and there was only the sound of bullfrogs croaking between the reeds.

"Johnny!" We all screamed his name. We stood in the mud on the edge of the dark water, screaming his name over and over. Looking at the pond was like looking into the night sky. Constellations glowed like scattered diamonds. Even the ripples disappeared. We hollered for Johnny as tears fell down our faces, but not a single one of us dared to dive in there and help him. Not a single one.

We ran from that pond like the devil himself was at our heels. Next day the county sheriff sent a diver in there to comb the pond, looking for Johnny's body. It made the headlines of all the local newspapers, but they never found so much as a little finger. Johnny was gone, just like Old Man Carter was gone. Carried deep into the earth by the thing in the pond.

Nobody went down there to hunt frogs again.

The old Carter house stood half-submerged at the pond's western edge. If you walked the dirt road that wound past it, you'd hear them frogs croaking and burping from the shattered windows of the house. Only frogs and toads lived in that old house now, and every kid in Ellot County new it was haunted.

My pa whupped me good for my part in Johnny's disappearance. He warned me I'd get worse if I ever went near that pond again. So I didn't. But I did see Johnny again a few months later. It was April and a big storm blew in, thunder and lightning and sheets of rain thick enough to drown a man in the street. I was in my bedroom reading *Tarzan and the Jewels of Opar*. Johnny had loaned me his dog-eared copy the week before he died, but I hadn't got around to reading it until now. I was so involved in the ape-man's adventures I forgot about all the storm. Ma and Pa were huddled by the fireplace in the livin' room with my little sister Sara. I was in another world altogether, a world of lost cities and deadly jungles, lost in the pages of my book.

Somebody knocked on my window. I looked up from the book, but the window was a grey mirror slick with raindrops. A pale shadow stood out there in the rain, something I could barely see. The knock wasn't loud, and I thought maybe I'd imagined it. But then it came again, low and insistent. Johnny Haxton used to knock on my window like that when he wanted me to sneak outside after dark. My first thought was "Johnny! He's still alive! He didn't die in that pond—he ran off. And now he's come back to tell me he's okay."

I went to the window and opened it to the pouring rain. Immediately I was soaked. It was cold, and the air stank of fish scales and worm flesh. A dark figure stood in the rain, about Johnny's height. He'd moved back from the window a ways, and the rain obscured his face. But I could tell it was Johnny Haxton. Same skinny arms, same wild hair, and the same knock on my window.

"Johnny?" I stuck my head halfway outside.

"It's me," he said. His voice was hoarse, like he had a mouthful of mud caught in his throat.

"You're alive?" I said. The rain splattered my face.

Johnny didn't say anything, just stood there in the cold rain. A different smell reached my nostrils, and it reminded me of a dead dog's carcass I had once seen rotting on the side of the road.

"I found him," Johnny said. I still couldn't see his face well. Thunder broke the sky above us.

"Found who?" I said, but I already knew.

"Old Man Carter," he said. I noticed he wasn't shivering at all.

"Come inside," I said. "Come sit by the fire."

Johnny raised a hand. "No," he said. "I gotta get back soon. I...I wanted to let you know."

"Let me know what?" I asked. "Where did you run off to?"

"Down there," he said. One of his bony fingers pointed to the sopping ground. "He's down there. Been down there all along."

"Down where?" I asked. My hair was soaked, and the rain wetted down my nightshirt. I shivered the way Johnny should have been shivering. The cold air was seeping into my room, along with the rotten smell. Something had died out there in the mud, a drowned rat, a dog, maybe a cat.

"It's wonderful, Teddy," Johnny said. "You have to see it. It's better than Opar. Better than Atlantis. Better than Camelot. Come with me… you'll see."

I shook my head. "Come inside, Johnny. I don't know what you're talkin' about."

"*Tsath*," Johnny said. "City of the Sleeping God. It's been there forever…longer than the United States…longer than Egypt…ever since the Great Cataclysm. The Children of Tsathoggua built it from sapphire and quartz. It's magnificent, Ted. And now they worship even stranger gods…"

"Tsathoggua?" I remembered the name from an issue of *Weird Tales*. "The frog-god? That ain't real, Johnny. It's just a story. Come inside and get warm now."

Johnny laughed, and his teeth chattered.

"Now why would I lie to my best buddy?" Johnny said. "I just want you to see it with your own eyes. To see *them*. Come with me now, and you'll never be cold again. This is your only chance…" Johnny reached out his hand and stepped closer to the window.

The lightning flashed and I saw his face. The skin was loose and pale about his skull, bloated and crisscrossed with blue veins. Black weeds hung tangled in his hair, and his clothing was nothing more than muddy rags. His eyeballs had fallen too far back in their sockets, and it was clear now that the rotting smell was him.

Johnny was dead after all, but somehow still walking and talking.

"Old Man Carter struck an underground river," Johnny said. Dark foam streamed from his shriveled lips as his lower jaw clacked. "The deep water pulled him right down and the current washed him all the way to K'n-yan. That's where they found his body—on the shore of the sunless sea."

I told Johnny to shut up. Tears streamed from my eyes even as the rain washed them away. His dead mouth kept on moving, and his words burned into my memories.

"They raised him up," Johnny said. "Now he serves them. There is no greater honor."

"I don't want to hear any more—"

"He came for me," Johnny said. "So they could raise me up too. Oh, you should see it. The towers of blue crystal, the domes bright as gold, alive with atomic fires. They move like angels in globes of light, drifting and flying and making love…they made us their slaves and now we'll never have to fear death again. What's there to be afraid of when you've already died? They raised us up, Ted! Come with me before it's too late! Let them raise you up!"

Johnny's hand came closer and I slammed the window shut. I must have screamed because Ma and Pa came rushing into my room. Ma told me later they found me crying and drenched on the floor by the window, but I don't remember that. They put me to bed and I lay in a fever for the next three days. I never told them about Johnny, or the things he said to me. I guess I figured nobody would believe me.

I never finished Johnny's book. I couldn't touch it anymore. Every time I tried, I'd see his swollen, rotting face on the page. *"They raised him up!"* He say it again in my dreams, or during moments of quiet contemplation. I started sneaking whiskey from my old man's stash to dull my dreams and still my racing thoughts. I think Ma knew I was drinking, but she didn't say a thing about it. The booze kept me calm.

A month later I dug through the attic and found that old copy of *Weird Tales*. I found the story that mentioned Tsathoggua. Supposedly it was a massive, toad-like entity who dwelled in a deep cavern beneath the earth during prehistoric ages. There was no description in that story of a fantastic underground city known as Tsath, but it did mention various pre-human races who worshipped the toad-god with sacrifices of living flesh. But this was just a story in a pulp magazine—the kind of publication my parents called "ungodly trash," and would throw into the fireplace if they got half a chance.

By winter I had convinced myself that Johnny's visit had been only a nightmare. I walked by the pond and it was frozen over, as it always was during the cold months. It seemed harmless under all that ice. I tried again but still couldn't finish the Tarzan book Johnny had given me. Eventually I dropped it into the fireplace, along with that copy of *Weird Tales*. I thought maybe burning them both would end my nightmares, and it worked for a while.

On the day I turned eighteen the local draft board let me know I was going to fight Nazis in Europe. The States had joined the war two years previous, and things weren't going too well over there. Sixteen young men from Ellot County entered the service that month, although some had volunteered for duty. It didn't matter—willingly or unwillingly—we shipped off to basic training, then to the battlefields of France.

The endless fear and trauma that comes with fighting a war kept me from thinking about Old Man Carter, his pond, or Johnny. At times I completely forgot about them. Sometimes, though, we'd march by a quiet little pond in the French countryside, and it all came back like a case of mental indigestion. Unlike the other fellas in my unit, I wouldn't swim in or drink from any ponds. I had no problem with free-flowing rivers, but I kept away from standing bodies of water as much as possible.

I remember sitting in camp one night, eating stew out of my helmet, imagining that every pond in the world was linked by a network of subterranean rivers, and that all of these rivers led to a sunless ocean that carried bones, jewels, and the bodies of dead men to the shore of K'n-yan. There, on sands bright as crushed sapphires, busy skeletons and restless mummies roamed about picking up useful and fascinating refuse for the Masters of Tsath. In the back of my mind, I saw the walking dead march from the sunless sea to the glittering spires of the toad-god's city. Among those diligent corpses I recognized the faces of Johnny Haxton and Old Man Carter, although how I recognized them in such a decayed state, I couldn't begin to say.

A buddy woke me up. I'd fallen asleep near the campfire while the rest of the unit bathed and splashed in a pond next to a burned-out French farmhouse. They teased me for a while about my fear of ponds, a terror so great it gave me mumbling nightmares. But I wasn't so sure my vision of Tsath had been a nightmare at all. It seemed as real as the war itself: A manifestation of impossible horrors made real. I didn't say anything like that out loud. I didn't want to get kicked out of the army as a nut-case.

One morning near Toulon a division of German forces ambushed us and killed half the unit. I took a bullet in the leg that left me lame, so I'd get out of the service honorably, not by virtue of insanity. I didn't want to go home. I didn't want to go back to Ellot County and Old Man Carter's pond. Still the power of that dark water pulled on me like a magnet. There was no escaping it.

"I know you want to stay here and see this out with your buddies," Captain Ross told me. "But it's time for you to go home. You're no good to us with a busted leg. Count your blessings, Ted. You did your part. Now go home and rest." I thought about the buddies who'd been killed next to me. I thought about the men I'd killed, either long-range or face-to-face. There were so many of them, I had lost count. I heard their screams again, the boom of the artillery. I cried in that hospital bed like I'd cried the night dead Johnny came to my window. The captain held onto my shoulders like a father would. He was a good man. The next day I began a series of flights that would take me back to the States. On that same day, Captain Ross went back to the front, where he took a German bullet in the head and died instantly. I found out about it when I opened a letter that had passed me on the way home.

Ma was sick with the cancer and wouldn't last much longer. Pa was taking it hard, hitting the bottle. My little sister was just old enough to care for them both. They were happy for a little while to have me home again, but they could tell I wasn't the same. I didn't talk much anymore, and when I did they cringed at the things I shared. Nobody wanted to hear about the war—not the bloody details, the spilled brains, the slaughtered children, the constant staring into the face of death until you were numb and half-dead yourself.

I'd been back for three days when I found myself limping by the old Carter place. It was high summer, hot and humid. The pond was still the same size, but its waters were darker now. The sunlight couldn't penetrate its surface at all. The old Carter house had fallen to rubble, half of it lying underwater. The cries of bullfrogs and toads filled the air, and I sat there until dark.

The moon rose full and round. I remembered looking at it from a battlefield five thousand miles away. Stand anywhere in the world and you'll see the same moon as everyone else. The moon is a constant, like Carter's pond. Now I saw the moon's reflection gleaming on the surface of the pond, and a sudden understanding washed over me. It all made sense. Before me lay the gateway to an eternal world where change was a myth and death a distant memory. I bent down to drink the cool water, and my tears added a pinch of salt to its sweetness. I waded in and floated on my back atop the water, the moon fixed in my vision like the answer to an unasked question.

I waited for Johnny to come back. Waited to be pulled low so I could be raised up.

I was ready now. Sometimes the waters rippled and bubbled around me, releasing odd vapors into the air. Sometimes I called Johnny's name, but it didn't do me any good.

Maybe I'd waited too long and the gate to K'n-yan was closed forever. Maybe I would never walk the glimmering streets of Tsath, where statues of the toad-god stood like stone behemoths above luminous ramparts.

Now they worship even stranger gods...

When the sun came up, I swam to the pond's edge and fell asleep. I woke up and went back to my folks' house to write all of this down on paper. People were bound to wonder about me like they wondered about Old Man Carter, and I wanted to explain things myself. I didn't show what I wrote to anyone yet. I knew better. They'd use it as evidence to lock me in a crazy-house.

Two nights later Ma died in her sleep. We buried her on the hill behind the house, and my father stopped talking to me. We drank together, but we didn't talk. My sister moved out of the house to live with a young man she'd been courting for a while. There was nothing else she could do for Pa and me.

Pa was still snoring when I got up this morning. I spent the last of my army pay on a case of good whiskey and left it for him on the dining room table. Then I hobbled over to the old Carter place and took a swim in the pond. Now and then deep rumblings came from below the water. I imagined scaly things swimming up from the sunless ocean with tongues extended like octopus tentacles, pulling me down, deep into the world below the world, where glorious Tsath awaited my service. Where Johnny's bones rambled along golden beaches gathering the detritus of mystery and carrying it back to enrich the treasure vaults of the Masters.

I floated on the black waters, reflected constellations swimming about me.

Still Johnny hasn't come for me. Neither has Old Man Carter.

I should have taken Johnny's invitation on that cold rainy night so many years ago. Now I have to do things the hard way.

I found a big rock in the pasture, as heavy a stone as I could carry. It didn't take long to weave some reeds into a sturdy rope. I tied one end to the rock and the other about my waist.

As soon as I finish writing this, I'll wade through the mud to the center and let the stone carry me down…down into the swirling depths of Carter's well…down into the rushing chaos of that nameless river…beyond that into the currents of the sunless ocean…and ultimately to the glittering shore of the toad-god's kingdom. When I close my eyes, I see the crystalline towers of Tsath rising toward a stalactite sky, where flocks of serpent-bats glide like sparrows. I see myself marching along the jeweled strand, once again part of a unit with a purpose. Fleshless and deathless beings with no more blood or tears to spill. One of them is my best friend.

Whoever finds this notebook has a choice. You can believe everything I've written, if you have a mind to. Or you can toss it into the fireplace like a worthless old pulp and watch it burn. Some folks just can't abide the truth. Especially when it's ugly. But for others the truth is all they have, no matter how bitter, strange, or unbelievable.

The black toads gather around me, croaking their ancient songs.

They know what's coming next.

See you soon, Johnny.

Enter The Cobweb Queen
by Adrian Cole

From the files of Nick Nightmare

Whenever I see mist, fog or smog, I immediately start wondering who's responsible. Yeah, the smart guys would say, the weather. Like I don't know that. I also know that thick, swirling vapors can also presage the coming of something supernatural, twisted, or hell-bent on wreaking havoc. When the noxious stuff is also slightly greenish in hue and contains more than a hint of a leering face or two, a gleam of teeth, then I know things are invariably going to get a little hairy. So when I ran into a wall of churning fog on my way to a rendezvous with Montifellini, he of Magic Bus fame, I gathered my wits about me and pulled my long coat tighter.

I'd had a cryptic note from him, telling me we should meet in a convenient side street, where he'd pick me up in his unique vehicle and whisk me off someplace where I'd hear something to my advantage. Like, how to prolong my existence, or avoid the unwanted advances of yet another alien intrusion. I have become the target of numerous dark and dubious powers in recent times. It would be nice to ignore them or project a few potent verbal discouragements their way, but sometimes you just have to get more physical. If Montifellini says there's trouble brewing, you need to pay heed.

I fought my way through the aerial blanket, barely able to keep my bearings, but sure enough, the Magic Bus was parked not far ahead, under a street lamp whose tired halo of light burned little brighter than a Zippo flame. The bus was a relic of the 1950s, a squat, snub-nosed vehicle, its paintwork a mixture of yellow and black. I heard the strains of Puccini billowing out from the bus, but don't ask me which of his works. Montifellini has done his best to educate me in matters operatic, but I'm more of a rock and blues man myself.

I clambered aboard. The big man smiled hugely. Well, he did most things hugely. He more than filled the driver's seat. He turned down the thundering orchestra and waved me aboard.

"What's on the menu tonight?" I asked him as he got his incredible machine moving.

"Someone wants to meet you, Nick. Says it's urgent. I think there may be some big problems coming your way."

"Why me?"

"Since when does the famous Mr Nightmare start asking dumb questions?"

I gripped the passenger support bar alongside the driver's cabin as the bus lurched and bounced. Already we were off the New York streets, that or this district was undergoing a minor quake. There was nothing outside but the fog, like we were rolling along a sea bottom. The Magic Bus goes anywhere, literally. Sometimes I reckon Montifellini could take you to Never Never Land if you asked him nicely.

"You heard of Ulthar?" he said.

"City of cats?" I dragged a few references from my brain, which was as fogged up as the world outside. It had been a long, tedious day, sorting through too much accumulated paperwork.

"That's it," he said. "I got my Bella there."

Bella was his cat, a particularly feisty calico, no-nonsense beastie, not to be messed with. She tolerated me, which made me privileged among men. I looked around the bus. Bella occasionally rode in it, but not on this trip. The bus was empty, save for me. If we were going to Ulthar, it figured. From what I'd heard, it wasn't somewhere you'd want to go without a damn good, probably weird, reason. Don't ask me what dimension Ulthar was in. You could spend a week speculating and drive yourself nuts.

"Who's the contact?" I asked.

"Guy named Long Tall Sonny. Traveler, musician, wheeler and dealer."

"A hobo."

"Sort of. He gets around. Learns things. Useful contact, you know?"

My world and those I slipped into in the course of my bizarre private eye existence was full of Long Tall Sonny's of one kind or another. Some were chancers, bottom-feeders living off scraps, others could be relied on to produce a nugget of information from time to time. Montifellini was no fool. No way would he drag me out into a place as off the beaten track as Ulthar unless it meant something, maybe the difference between life and death. So he gave Long Tall Sonny some credibility.

Eventually we parked up in deathly silence, still enshrouded in fog. I could see buildings around us, distorted by the swirling clouds, although these buildings would have been damn weird in normal light. This was Ulthar, a place of narrow streets and alleys, winding up and down at generally dizzy angles, its houses twisted as if they'd been thrown together in a storm, packed and piled.

"Welcome to the Dreamlands," said Montifellini. "You want an inn called the *Skai Arms*. It's at the top of that incline. Your watch working? Okay, come back within two hours. I'll be here to take you home."

I disembarked and climbed the jumble of stone steps. It wasn't easy because they seemed to have been designed to make you dizzy and direct you anywhere but your destination. Behind me, Montifellini ground his gears and the Magic Bus was quickly swallowed by more billows of fog. It might have been night time. There were lamps, but for all I knew they burned perpetually in this dismal city. As I went up, hemmed in by leaning houses seemingly on the point of collapse, I noticed shapes slinking about me, just out of clear vision. Ulthar was famed for its innumerable felines, a host beyond number. They prowled and purred and suffered visitors on the clear understanding that one step out of line would be punished with feral fury, something I was not prepared to put to the test.

I reached the inn, identified by a low-hanging sign, its paint faded and flaking. Stooping, I entered its shadowy embrace. Inside it was spacious, with a high ceiling. A big hearth and a glowing fire made it more welcoming than the drab streets. I pushed through the empty chairs and tables to the bar.

"You from the Southlands?" said the barman. He welcomed me as cheerily as he would have a strong head cold. His rheumy eyes regarded me suspiciously.

I glared back at him. "Nope. Never mind where I'm from, pal. I'm looking for a guy named Long Tall Sonny. Or maybe I should say, he's looking for me."

"I don't want no trouble." As he spoke, I saw shapes shifting around him, on shelves, along the bar, on some of the tables—cats. Scores of them. Every one of the furry beasts was looking directly at me, wide-eyed and intimidating. Some of them were as big as a small dog. All in all there were a lot of teeth in that place. I heard a communal purring, which somehow seemed to form itself into a soft, rising chant, focused around one word. Food.

"Sooner you get him outta here—and his freaky friend—the better," the barman grumbled.

Friend? Two of them. I didn't order a drink, just followed directions as the barman pointed to a shadowy corner of the inn, where a figure slumped over a table. Drunk? Hell, that was all I needed. I went over to the man and he looked up nervously. He was skin and bone wrapped up in rags, with a gaunt face suggesting he wasn't too familiar with the concept of healthy eating. As I stood by his table he shivered and curled up tighter.

"Long Tall Sonny?" I said.

He nodded until I thought his head would drop off. "Did Montifellini send you?" he squawked.

"Yeah. You got something for me? I don't have a lot of time." As I spoke I caught movement behind him in deeper shadows, and I brought out one of my Berettas in a fast draw.

Long Tall Sonny reached out with a hand—more like a claw—and gripped my wrist. "It's okay," he said. "I can explain."

I tried to get a clearer view of whoever had moved back there, but all I saw was a blurred shadow and a pair of eyes. Very green, bright and sparkling. My guess was, it was a dame.

"She's my—my, uh, partner," said Long Tall Sonny. He didn't seem very sure. "We need to get back to New York. Your New York, and mine. Otherwise they'll kill us."

"And what do I get out of it?"

"I'll tell you everything. Just get us away before it's too late. The Cobweb Queen knows I'm here in Ulthar. She's closing in."

I didn't know of any Cobweb Queen, but anyone who knows me will tell you I'm not a big fan of spiders, or anything on eight legs, or even six for that matter. To be blunt, I'm not that fond of two-legged beings either. I thought I heard a change in the tone of the moggie collective, a sort of growling. They didn't like spiders, either. I recalled that Montifellini's cat, Bella, occasionally found one and chewed on it, a snack between meals.

Long Tall Sonny lowered his hand, but I kept the gun aimed at the shadow person. My eyes had adjusted to the darkness and I saw now it was someone in a thick, black cloak, hooded and with a black scarf covering its face, save those eyes. They were the only thing about it that moved.

"So—convince me I should help you."

"The Cobweb Queen is a cruel mistress," said Long Tall Sonny. "She's enslaved half a world and she's always greedy for more. There were three of them once, demi-gods. They were sisters, the last of their race, but they fought the Old Ones, the terrible deities from the stars, and lost. Two were destroyed, burned to cinders by the wrath of Azathoth. The Cobweb Queen escaped and started a new empire of her own. Zermillia wants out."

By Zermillia I guessed he meant the green-eyed shadow behind him.

"We want to get to the safety of New York. The Cobweb Queen can't get through to it. Her movements are restricted by the servants of the Old Ones."

"Well, that's good to know."

"Zermillia and me will start a new life together."

It was tough imagining anyone starting a new life with this bundle of bones, but who was I to argue with love? It being blind, and all.

"If you get us back, we can help make sure the defenses are strengthened. Just in case the Cobweb Queen tries to invade. She's restricted, but she's powerful. Block her out on your side and she'll never get through. She'll look someplace else for new conquests."

Before I could poke him for more information, the feline tribe set up a new caterwauling. Something had spooked them, big time. The barman rushed to one of the tiny windows and peered outside. Whatever was out there had upset the apple-cart. He swung round and looked at me angrily. "You brought them! You treacherous -" He ran off a string of uncomplimentary insults that made me wince.

I ignored him and went to the dusty window. One look out explained the barman's over-excitement. Several figures stood in the street, contemplating the inn. I would have said they were men, but they looked more like they'd risen from the deeps of the Black Lagoon. They were naked, had obvious gills, eyes like moons and a spine of sharp quills that ran from the back of their heads to the lower end of their backs. And being a dark shade of green added to the aquatic effect.

"No friends of mine," I said.

Long Tall Sonny yelped in horror and started gabbling. "They serve the Old Ones! They've come for Zermillia. They want to trap the Cobweb Queen and sacrifice her. You don't know what they'll do to her. We have to get away!"

"Let's not get hysterical." I turned to the barman. "This is the part where I ask you if there's a back way out of here. Maybe you could have your cats distract those fish-suckers?"

He seemed to understand that me and my two new pals weren't quite as undesirable as he'd originally imagined, whereas the shamblers outside were all that and more. He nodded and spoke to the mass of cats, which had miraculously grown to about three times its original size. Boy, were those beasts ready for action. The barman swung open the door and the cats poured out, shrieking as only cats can. I didn't stay to watch the bloody rending and tearing that followed. Long Tall Sonny stood up, a spindly guy who must have been nigh on six foot six. He had a battered old guitar hanging from a shoulder strap. Both had seen better days, better years even.

The barman led the three of us through the inside of the pub and to a low doorway that opened to another alley. He gave us instructions so I could find our way back to the original steps that would drop down to where the Magic Bus would be waiting. On our way, I could hear the frenzied sounds of wild animals at war and was thankful I couldn't see any of it. We got back to the stair, but not before I sensed other shapes out in the fog, like smears in the swirling clouds. They were closing in. This was going to be a close shave.

Mercifully the unmistakable shape of Montifellini's vehicle was waiting. I hurried Long Tall Sonny and Zermillia towards it. She'd managed to run the gauntlet still mummified in her cloak, apparently as easy on her feet as if she'd been gliding. I heard the scuffling of many feet behind us. Things were undoubtedly closing in and I smelt the salty stink of the sea.

I flung open the door of the bus. Montifellini looked down from his seat, his black eyebrows raised in an expression of deep curiosity. "You're in a hurry, my friend."

"Two more passengers," I said. "Can we scoot, pronto?"

He revved the engine, which made a sound suggestive of something about to blow itself apart. But the bus was alive, primed. I gestured for Long Tall Sonny to get aboard and he did so, Zermillia behind him. Her head was down as she drifted past the huge driver, not wanting to look at him, or be seen. I got on board and shut the door. Long Tall Sonny and Zermillia went into the empty bus and sat near the back, looking out of the windows at the thickening gloom.

I stood beside Montifellini as he took us away. I thought I felt something bump on the sides of the bus, like we were being mobbed, in danger of being turned over. Montifellini shouted a few choice Italian swearwords and I picked out the word 'paintwork'. Then we were plunging into a new fog bank, dark as a tunnel.

"Passengers?" said Montifellini. "I recognize Long Tall Sonny. But who's the other?"

I attempted to explain.

"Something is wrong," he said, his voice low, covered by the rumble of the engine. "Have you seen her clearly?"

"No, we didn't have a lot of time for introductions, not with the fishy tribe about to organize a three course meal."

"You say she was a servant of the Cobweb Queen? I know a little about that monster. Nasty lady, if that's what she is, my friend. Her servants are not women you would want to associate with. Even you would draw the line, I think."

"Hey, easy on the compliments," I grunted. "I've just had a run of bad luck with the fairer sex of late, that's all."

He grinned. "Sure." His grin dissolved. "Seriously, Nick, we're in trouble. We need a little time to work this out. Go and sit with them. Find out what you can."

I did so. Long Tall Sonny was hunched up, not very talkative. Zermillia's vivid eyes studied the fog as if it would reveal its secrets to her.

"Tell me about your former mistress," I said, but she shrank back as if I'd threatened her. I wasn't going to get anything out of her, obviously. So I sat back and let the bus wind its way back to my world.

* * * *

We'd stopped. It was night outside, and still foggy as hell.

"Terminus!" called Montifellini.

I went up front. "Seriously?" I said, voicing my skepticism.

"The fog will pass. Go and get some sleep. Tuck the lovers up in bed." He said it with a tone of finality and I knew that was it. Out. Resolve whatever problems I'd now gleaned from this little jaunt without him. I grunted and waved Long Tall Sonny to me. He and his cloaked partner disembarked and the three of us watched the Magic Bus rumble away, its exhaust pumping out clouds of fumes that suggested it was where the fog had originated. Maybe it had. Montifellini works in mysterious ways.

"Where are we?" said Long Tall Sonny.

"Good question."

"This doesn't feel like our New York."

I wasn't going to argue. Instead I watched the fog as it began to close in again, tight as a fist. I heard the sound of lapping water and a sudden gust brought with it a distinctive fetor of sea. So we were on a quayside. I turned to see Long Tall Sonny and the woman walking away. I followed them.

Ahead of us a number of buildings reared up, partially obscured by darkness and mist. Blocks of stone, windowless and in places overhung with thick tresses of leaves, ivy maybe, or some kind of matted climbers. This place was deserted and had been for a long time. My guess was, a very long time. There were stone steps leading up to an open rectangle of deeper darkness, a door. Further up the quay a long slipway dropped at an angle into the mist and again I heard water lapping at it. There'd been no ships sliding down that ramp in an age.

I paused at the top of the steps, looking around. If this was New York, I was a monkey's uncle. Where the heck had Montifellini dropped us—and why?

Long Tall Sonny re-emerged from the building. "Zermillia's gone inside, looking for somewhere to crash until sunrise. Where is this place?"

"The truth is, I don't know. It's not our Big Apple."

He let out a deep breath of relief. "I'm cool with that."

"You want to explain why?"

"It's Zermillia." He dropped his voice. "She's not my partner. Well, she sort of is. She seduced me. I feel kinda impelled to do what she tells me. She has powers. She's not on the run from the Cobweb Queen."

"You're not making my night any better."

"She's a Summoner." He peered through the doorway, listening. When he was satisfied we were still out of the girl's earshot, he spoke again. "The Cobweb Queen has eight of them, her most powerful servants. They look for new places for her, like scouting bees. When they find somewhere, they perform certain rituals and summon her into existence. Right now the Cobweb Queen is heavily pregnant. When she arrives, she'll discharge her countless thousands of offspring and the invasion will begin."

"Invasion?"

"New world, new home, new beginning."

"And is there any good news?"

"What you just told me. This isn't our New York. And Zermillia doesn't know that. Better if she doesn't."

I was beginning to get the picture—and Montifellini had indeed cottoned on to something. Which is why he dumped us here. Not like him to abandon me, though. Maybe he thought I'd wriggle out. Right now, though, I didn't have a key.

What I did have, tucked inside my coat, was a flashlight. I pulled it out, as well as one of my guns, and switched on. The beam shed light beyond the doorway as we entered. This was some place, a granddaddy of a warehouse, its ceiling way up above us, festooned with more creepers, lianas, jungle plants. Another piece of this weird puzzle clicked into place. This wasn't just a case of where we were, it was also *when* we were. My guess was, a long time ago. Montifellini had done a good job of shipwrecking us.

The walls were coated with slime, fungus, mold, you name it, and it was soon apparent I didn't need my flash. Some of this stuff glowed, a baleful candle-light that threw everything into relief. We'd climbed more steps to the central area and could have been in a primitive cathedral, its tall columns angled upwards, some leaning, others collapsed, but still enough to keep most of the roof up. Tendrils of fog curled around up there, feeling their way in through an open section, but quickly dissipating as they groped about in the inner air, a bizarre, natural defense.

Long Tall Sonny gasped, a skeletal, bony hand indicating one of the walls, where an inscription had been embossed and could still be read. To me it was gibberish, as intelligible as Sanskrit, but he recognized it. He was a travelling man, so maybe he'd picked a few things up on his ramblings.

"Jehoshaphat!" he cried, then dropped his voice again. "I think I know where we are. It's an island, an old kingdom. One of a number of places sacred to…an old religion."

I wasn't exactly loving this. An alien world, a remote time, and we were on a goddamn *island*. "Something tells me you're not talking High Anglican Church."

He pointed to some crude carvings, bizarre figures cavorting about, figures with gills, spatulate hands, piscean features. Not unlike the things I'd seen shambling about in Ulthar.

"Servants of the sea god," he said, shuddering.

"Azathoth? Is that what you called it?"

He shook his head. "Azathoth is at the heart of his own universe, linked to many others, a sort of primal chaos, a cosmic being beyond understanding, who -"

"I get the picture. So which god are we talking about here?"

"He who dwells in the deep ocean. There is a theory that his city, R'Lyeh, sits in more than one dimension, on more than one world. This is one of them. It's out there, in the fathomless ocean chasms, where he dreams. This citadel is one of a number that ring the ocean, a place where his children can gather, swarming up from the waters."

"So, all in all, pal, this is probably the worst place in any number of universes for us to be. Sandwiched between the water god and the spider monster." I was thinking, the next time I saw Montifellini, I was going to have a few words with the big guy. Was he nuts? Then it hit me. No, not completely. There was method in his madness. Things started to make sense, the internal fog clearing if the stuff outside wasn't.

"And all this you've told me," I said to Long Tall Sonny, "Would be news to Zermillia? She doesn't know where, or when, we are?"

"It's better if she doesn't. But ask her yourself. She's coming."

We were almost in the center of the huge building, dwarfed by its monumental stones, its floor a series of concentric mosaics, ancient patterns. Zermillia came out of the shadows beyond it. She had got rid of her cloak, hood and facial mask. I tried not to gape. She looked like something that had stepped off a catwalk in the latest Parisian fashion show. She wore a single, flowing garment, a very pale pink affair that hugged most of her contours, thin as silk. Her hair was as white as snow, a tumbling mass, and her skin was also white. An albino, as pure as I'd ever seen. Her face was human and yet had an elfish look, if I can put it that way. Her eyes were a brilliant green, emphasized now by that white skin, and her lips were very full, blood red, though that wasn't lipstick. Beauty incarnate, and yet in a way repellent, at least to me. Long Tall Sonny had already succumbed to her charms. His natural inclination wasn't to recoil, far from it.

"Mr Stone, or should I say, Nick Nightmare," she purred. The cats of Ulthar would have liked that. "Good of you to help us."

"Always like to keep the clients satisfied."

Her green eyes surveyed me coolly and I was thinking more of serpents than spiders. "I am a little puzzled, though. This building, its location—aren't we a little off the beaten track?"

I could feel Long Tall Sonny's terror crawling up him from his boots like a hot flush of plague. His long face was slick with sweat. Panic was poking him.

"That's right, ma'am. We're in New York, but this is about as insalubrious a spot as I could find."

Those crimson lips made a little moue. "Quite. And why did you choose it?"

"Thing is, ma'am—"

"Zermillia."

"Sure. Thing is, guys like me who travel around in ways most folks don't even know about, are secretive types. Only a few of us have the keys to the kind of trip you just made."

"Yes, it's why my mistress selected you."

"We come and go privately. If we'd walked out into Times Square in broad daylight, well, we'd have caused a stir. My guess is, your mistress would rather announce her coming when it suits her. Element of surprise." I waved my arms at the surrounding stone. "No one will know she's here until she's ready."

"Very clever, Mr Nightmare. Your point is well taken."

I thought I'd done pretty well for an on-the-hoof explanation. But we were a long way from being out of the woods yet.

"What is this place?" she asked innocently.

"Uh, well, ma'am—Zermillia—it's an old building. There was a war many years ago, a world war, in fact, and our military powers built a whole lot of warships, some in secret bases like this one, to disguise the scale of the work. Even in its heyday, this place was remote, out on the edge of New York. When the war ended, it was abandoned. Never been used since. We're probably the first people to set foot here in a long time. So we're not likely to be disturbed." All this was complete bull, but experience has taught me the key to bull is to deliver it with conviction.

"The Cobweb Queen will be delighted. We shall begin the rituals after dawn. I suggest you get some rest. It will be quite taxing."

"I assume you won't be needing us."

She smiled her chilling smile and I mean icy. "Oh, I will, Mr Nightmare. You and Sonny are an integral part of the—ceremony." She left us again, swallowed by the walls of shadow.

"Dawn," I said to him. "That could be a problem."

"We have to get out of here," Long Tall Sonny muttered.

"When dawn comes up, and if the fog has lifted, it won't be the Manhattan skyline she sees across the water. My guess is, it'll be jungle. Not a concrete one. One with a whole lot of trees. And we're not talking weeping willows."

* * * *

We snatched some uneasy sleep. My dreams were twisted ones, mostly to do with water and things bubbling up from it. Not helped by the sloshing and gurgling of the tide outside, sluicing up the big ramp. I heard things wading around in it, but with any luck that was just my fevered imagination. Who was I kidding?

Dawn came, its first light seeping through the east end of the building. The door through which we'd entered was shut, a solid block of stone sealing up the way out. Close by it, where the long slipway to the sea came into the building, I could see the outline of a huge door, its outline picked out in places as sunlight poked through the cracks of time. Maybe I'd been right about ships being launched from here, but whatever types of ships they'd been remained a mystery. No bad thing.

Long Tall Sonny and I got to our feet at the same time. Zermillia was watching us from the steps, a smile on her face that would have melted bronze. No doubt she was eager to get on with the summoning. Montifellini's devious plans were clearer to me now: have the Cobweb Queen brought here and virtually imprisoned. That was okay by me. The problem was, I didn't want to share her splendid isolation. I couldn't believe Montifellini would simply sacrifice me to achieve his aims. So I assumed he'd pick me up once the work was done.

Zermillia had been busy in the night. The huge chamber had a central area which she'd cleared of any debris, and she must have used a makeshift broom from some of the bigger leaves to sweep away the dust of the ages. What had been revealed on the circular floor was an intricate concentric sequence of glyphs, dancing figures and stars, a kind of pictographic saga hinting at a cosmic link between the world and the stars. I'd seen this kind of thing before, mainly in conjunction with the sea and certain things that shambled up from its deeps from time to time and mingled with the human population, not necessarily to its advantage.

Zermillia saw my expression and laughed, a cold sound that bounced around the high walls. "It's ironic," she said. "This abandoned temple to dead gods and the forgotten remnants of the Queen's enemies. It seems fitting that she will be brought here, hidden from your world in this shell."

So she hadn't bought my World War Two warship blarney. But she did think it was my world. I wish the thought had comforted me.

"Once," she went on, "the priests of another cult stood here and poured their libations to the Old Ones, summoning powers from the stars. I shall open another conduit. The Cobweb Queen will come, carrying her thousand young! Here they will bloom and go out into your city and feast! Days of great joy are upon us." She pointed to Long Tall Sonny, her finger a long, white stick, its nail as red as her lips. "Stand inside the circle!"

He snapped upright as if something had grabbed him. I could see him struggling against it, shaking like a doll caught in the mouth of a huge dog. It was hopeless—he couldn't prevent himself from being dragged across the circles to their innermost point. Zermillia lifted her arms and spoke to the heavens, and a scarlet mist surrounded her, its fingers reaching out and ripping Long Tall Sonny's ragged clothing off him. Naked, he looked even more bony, his flesh pale, his limbs like thin branches. Gasping with pain, he dropped to his knees, head bowed. His guitar rattled on the floor beside him.

I pulled out my twin Berettas and directed them at Zermillia.

"Save you bullets," she said. "They won't work on me. Enjoy your freedom for a while longer. Then prepare to meet your goddess."

She raised her hands again and now began a low dirge, her voice echoing in the chamber, rising in pitch, picked up by the acoustics and amplified. I'd seen gates opened before by songs, and although this one was quintessentially weird, its power became evident as something high above groaned and shifted, as if huge stones had been moved to let in daylight. Well, not daylight. It may have been daylight outside the building, but whatever conduit Zermillia had opened did so onto a black, starlit sky. As the song swelled, the stars were gradually blotted out by a vast bulk, a huge *something* coming over the roof. Its long, long legs, several of them, were as thick as palm trunks, hairy and fibrous. The Cobweb Queen was answering the summons.

Long Tall Sonny had collapsed and the invisible forces that gripped him twisted him until he was spread-eagled. I had a good idea what was coming next, and it was not going to be a pretty sight. Darkness descended, along with something else, something I first thought was gloopy, hanging in slick festoons. Cobwebs! Dozens of lengthy strands, unfurling like drapes. I was caught in a nasty dilemma. I wanted the Cobweb Queen snared in the trap, but not at the expense of Long Tall Sonny. Sure, he was a bit of a creep and I didn't owe him any favors—he'd dragged me into this mess in the first place—but it seemed wrong to let him become, presumably, a light snack for the grandmother of spiders.

So I fired off a couple of rounds at Zermillia, gambling that it was too late for the Queen to rise up and away again. I was right—her immense bulk kept lowering itself down into the chamber. The bullets *whanged* up against whatever shield Zermillia had erected around herself and I saw them spinning in mid-air, quickly cocooned in webbing like flies. Zermillia's song was unbroken, her face beatific, eyes on her mistress. I could hear Long Tall Sonny's guitar thrumming, as if he was playing it—he wasn't—and its chords complementing Zermillia's song.

Impotently I fired another few rounds as I backed away. A couple of the bullets hit the far wall of the chamber and ricocheted around the place like mad wasps. Incredibly they kept going, longer than I would have expected, like they'd picked up on the power that was in play and were accelerating. The sound as they bounced from wall to wall rose.

Zermillia stopped singing, the bulbous Cobweb Queen a dozen feet or so from the chamber's floor. I got a better view of the monster and gaped. It was no normal spider, and had an exaggerated head, shaped like a huge skull and—features. That face, it was stretched across the skull, but it was

Zermillia's face, or the prototype of it. Its brilliant, green eyes opened and fixed on me. I shrank back as if Satan himself had favored me with his sulfurous gaze.

Zermillia watched the buzzing bullets, then flung something at them, white light in jagged forks. There was a crackling, a hiss, something small rolling across stone, and the bullets were still, little smoking pellets, redundant. Zermillia stepped out of the circle and away from Long Tall Sonny, whose eyes were tightly closed, his body rigid.

My guess was Zermillia was about to taunt me and start in on me with her powers, with a view to divesting me of my clothes as she had done her earlier victim, but something checked her. Her head rose and she cocked her ears like a hunting eagle, picking up sounds outside the normal human range of hearing. I heard nothing—at first. Then it came to me, that soft whispering, a susurration. The sea outside. Lapping up against the huge doors. That and something else.

Visitors.

I worked my way back towards the base of the doors, to one side of the ramp. Zermillia wasn't impressed and flung even more of her light bolts my way. Behind her, the Cobweb Queen, the size of a house, blotted out the light, her legs stretching across the chamber. Long Tall Sonny was in shadow, but his fate was even more clear.

Beside me, light exploded and small sections of stone burst apart as Zermillia vented her petulance on me. In her irritation she'd damaged a lower part of the doors, and sunlight flooded in. That wasn't all that flooded in. A score of aquatic shapes rode in on the gush of sea water. They gave a whole new meaning to the concept of surfing. More of the door opened. I don't know what force was outside, dragging at it, and to be honest, I didn't want to, but it was enough to admit a whole host of these salty invaders.

Zermillia screamed in a combination of fury and fear. I liked the fear bit. I saw her make a break for the far end of the chamber. Meanwhile the Cobweb Queen shook herself and I saw her abdomen ripple then let loose a flood of smaller arachnid shapes. They may have been her babies, but they were the size of wolf hounds. And to add to their horrific appearance, they all had bloated quasi-human heads. And all their faces were replicas of Zermillia's. They scampered forward at speed, preparing to meet the onslaught of the water things. These were humanoid, having our general shape and limbs, but other than that they were more like crustaceans or fish, their limbs ending in claws that would have chopped a normal man in half. And those mouths! Looked like they were chewing on a nest of lampreys. I shrank back into what shadows I could find and mercifully I was ignored. The presence of the Cobweb Queen and her horrible spawn had driven the sea folk insane with anger and blood-lust. They broke on them like a huge wave and the conflict that ensued was violent and murderous. I had no idea what the outcome would be.

Fortunately Long Tall Sonny was as interesting to the sea things as I was, and at last he was able to break free of the power that had gripped him. He snatched up the remnants of his clothes, put them on, and regathered his dignity, as well as his now silent guitar. I waved him over to me and we stood, temporarily mesmerized by the confusion. We lost sight of Zermillia, but my guess was she was either buried under a mass of writhing tentacles and claws, or she'd found a back way out of there. I didn't much care one way or the other.

I dragged Long Tall Sonny out through the door into daylight. The churning sea was right up the slipway and for the moment had finished disgorging the horde of things from under its waves. There was a narrow path, a rough quay to one side and we edged along it. I looked out to sea. As I thought, no city skyline, but no jungle either, just a flat sea horizon. This island may not be anywhere near the mainland at all. Out in the bay, the deeper waters boiled. It looked like something even bigger and nastier was preparing its own version of a D-Day landing.

I shoved Long Tall Sonny along the quay and we kept going. Eventually, rounding the last of a series of rock outcrops, we came to a small bay and a bigger quay. There were buildings, small and cramped, but long abandoned. And no city.

"You okay?" I asked my companion.

"Thanks," he said. "You saved my bacon."

"Pal, you *were* the bacon. And we're not out of this yet."

* * * *

We spent the day waiting. I'd convinced myself Montifellini would come. Somehow that crazy bus of his would roll up on the quay and whisk us back to our saner world. Long Tall Sonny was skeptical. He shuddered every time we heard a distant boom as the conflict inside the old buildings raged on insanely. The sea hurled its waves at us, probably stirred up by events, but we were otherwise left alone. I didn't think we'd be safe indefinitely, though. Whoever won that clash of the Titans would seek us out eventually. A snack for the Cobweb Queen or a watery trip to R'Lyeh or some such tourist spot down in the deeps.

Evening finally turned up and my eyes, tired from scanning the emptiness of the sea, picked something up, a shape on the water, coming around the shoulder of rock to the west of us. A little craft, with one occupant. I slipped out a gun, fully loaded once more. As the canoe-like craft got closer, the figure waved cheerily. I knew the grinning face.

"Fred the Ferryman," I breathed. "That's a relief."

"You know him?"

"I'm happy to say yes." I helped Fred tie up at the quayside.

The little man's blob of a head bobbed up and down as he laughed. "Mr Stone. Montifellini told me I'd find you here. He'd have come himself, but there's an ocean of aquatic horrors on the lookout for him in this realm. And he was grumbling about some of them denting the bodywork of his bus. You know how that kind of thing irks him."

Long Tall Sonny looked a mite queasy. "You mean I have to get aboard? I get seasick."

I gave him my searching look. "Is it my imagination, or do I smell bacon?"

* * * *

Long Tall Sonny took his mind off the rocking of the boat as Fred ferried us through yet more banks of fog (which he breathed in happily) by strumming a few blues tunes on his guitar, while Fred added the lyrics, most of which centred around his having woken up that morning. No one was seasick, but I grumbled about the interminable fog, even if it did mask us from anything swimming about below us.

Some time later we bumped up against something and I realized we had arrived at yet another quayside. Long Tall Sonny and I climbed the weed-infested steps and up to dry-ish land. Fred gave us a cheery wave and rowed away, still singing about his baby having left him, though the event, if not a fiction, must have been a happy one. I wouldn't be buying the album.

"Are we home?" said my companion.

"I think we have one more trip to make." I pointed at a large, humped shadow. It shook to the strains of *Carmen*. Montifellini's Magic Bus was parked alongside some weird buildings that could only have been erected in Ulthar, to which we had apparently returned. "Let's get aboard. I want a few words with Pavarotti's cousin, several times removed."

Before we'd taken a few steps, things materialized in the fog on either side of us. Unpleasant things. Things that had lately been in that choppy sea, now sloping along, claws flexing, tentacular mouths wriggling, eager to fix on human flesh, specifically mine and Long Tall Sonny's. It was touch and go as to whether we'd make it to the bus before they fell on us. A wild screeching shattered the silence and the fog disgorged yet more shapes, to wit a seething mass, furry and feline. Cats, scores of them. In their forefront and yowling with maniacal fury, was none other than Montifellini's little calico heroine, Bella. She arched her back, her fur fluffed up and her tail three times as fat as normal, swishing to and fro like a conductor's baton directing her musical ensemble.

The sea spawn hissed, a sound nowhere near as effective as the terrifying caterwauling, and at once the battle began, while Long Tall Sonny and I edged closer and closer to the bus and its swelling chorus of toreadors. We tried not to watch as claws of varying sizes swiped at flesh and needle teeth sank into skin and scales. The walls of the buildings echoed to the concatenation of horrible sounds. We reached the door to the vehicle and I looked up to see the big man, sitting back, eyes closed in euphoric pleasure as he accompanied the lusty Italian singing booming from his speakers.

He opened an eye and favored me with a face-splitting grin. "Nick! I knew you'd get through. Come aboard, and bring your musical maestro with you."

We needed no second bidding as the battle on the quay, which had now assumed war proportions, snarled and hissed very close to the bus. Like the opera, it reached a crescendo—then stopped. There was only the fog. And a single cat. Bella. Insouciantly, she climbed up the steps into the bus, favored us with one of those imperious cat glances, found a comfortable seat and proceeded to wash herself as if nothing had happened.

"She is a Boudicca among cats," said her master proudly. "I take it you dealt with the intruder," he added, closing the door and wrestling the engine into life.

I was too relieved to be on board to make a big deal of it all. Long Tall Sonny sat down and idly picked at the strings of his guitar. "You know, that tune Zermillia was singing. Really melodic. Could be a winner."

I glared at him. "Sonny, you play *one note* of that song and I will remove both your arms and shove the guitar where the sun don't shine. Stick to twelve bar blues, okay?"

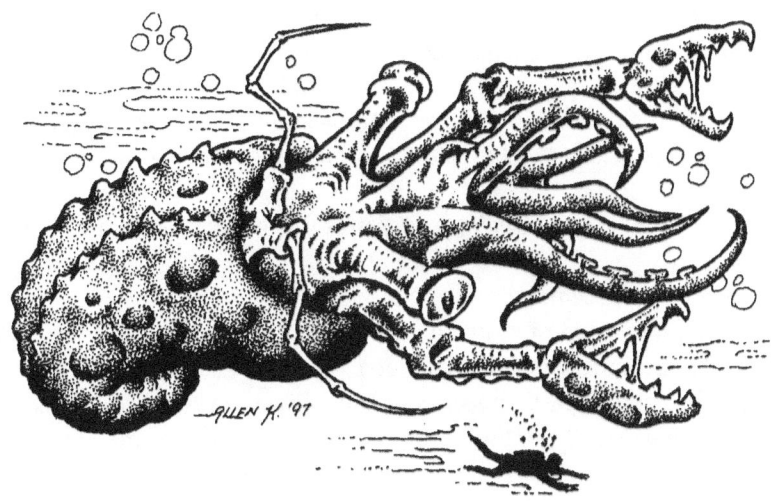

Tricks No Treats
by Paul Dale Anderson

One does not venture onto the streets of Arkham after dark on All-Hallow's Eve. I've been told that those who do, never return.

Or they come back totally and hopelessly mad.

Life-long residents remain safely ensconced inside their dilapidated homes, with all the doors securely bolted and windows shuttered tight. Outside, blustery fall winds wail and shriek through clogged eaves and denuded trees like crazed banshees. Dogs growl and howl.

Above the town, a huge flock of agitated whippoorwills—inexplicably delayed from migrating south for the winter and tonight sounding more like carrion-consuming birds of prey than delicate songbirds—issue incessant cries from dusk to dawn. Only the insane would go outside on a night like this or dare answer the door. I am not insane.

Nor am I the ignorant country bumpkin native New Englanders consider me to be as I wander deserted streets alone. I hold dual doctorates—one in archaeology and the other in arcane literature from the University of Chicago—and I have accompanied fellow Oriental Institute researchers to the farthest reaches of the accessible world.

I know many strange things, some of which were hidden from mankind for countless aeons before my colleagues and I unearthed them.

Which is the very reason I'm drawn, like a moth flirting with the tall flame flickering mesmerizingly atop a half-melted candle, to this hideously dark and desolate street in Arkham, Massachusetts, on this cold and blustery October 31st, near the end of the second decade of the third millennium of the modern era.

I have come tonight to discern for myself if what I've learned is really true.

Or merely a dream.

Antiquarian researches uncovered anecdotal evidence that certain occult locales become gateways between worlds at auspicious times when the heavens and our earth are strategically aligned. Allegedly among them are Stonehenge on the morning of the summer solstice; the Intihuatana of Machu Picchu at sunrise on the winter solstice, which is their summer solstice in the Southern Hemisphere; the three Great Pyramids of Giza when they align precisely with the three brightest stars of Orion's belt on the night of May eve; and, not far from the rare book collection of Miskatonic University's library, wherein lies the dreaded Necronomicon, the Old Witch House where Keziah Mason had once lived and where, at precisely midnight on Halloween, veils between worlds are thinnest.

There may be other places with portals to connect unseen worlds with our own. For all I know, somewhere in this world each and every night a different doorway briefly opens. Similar to worm holes, these are actually more like massive bank vault doors that automatically lock and unlock only when corresponding stars, not unlike tumblers of some cosmic combination lock, perfectly align.

Nor have I a clue how an obscure and allegedly-mad Arabian poet, astrologer, mathematician, and alchemist by the name of Abdul Alhazred discerned secret combinations of both past and future more than twelve centuries ago when neither Arkham nor the Witch House yet existed. Some scholars conjecture he was acting as a conduit between the remote past and the far future, that his fevered automatic scribblings ensued while in a fugue or trance state outside of time itself. It's even been suggested, by those susceptible to believe such nonsense, that he channeled the dreams of demons.

I come to Arkham tonight not only as a scientist eager to confirm research findings, but as a man hungry to glimpse once more the face of his beloved wife who shuffled off her mortal coil much too young and much too soon while I was away doing research. For I fervently believe, as did the ancients, that on this night when the veils are thinnest and the lines and angles between stars and planets are aligned exactly right, the dead may walk and talk again and be seen and heard by mortal man.

To be able to see and possibly even—dare I hope?—touch Laura again is worth any risk. I don't believe in the existence of boogeymen or demons. But I do believe our essences hasten someplace after death. Where that is, I hope to discover tonight in Arkham.

Although the old Witch House is gone—demolished by time and a superstitious citizenry who refused to build again on that cursed spot—a strange configuration of standing stones still remains on an island in the Miskatonic not far from the Garrison Street bridge. Just as ancient hands fashioned stones at Avebury and Stonehenge, the Intihuatana at Machu Picchu, and the Great Pyramids at Giza, so too did ancient hands position those stones in the Miskatonic to point to a secret doorway connecting the land of the living with the land of the dead.

As I stand atop the bridge, I hear ritual drumming off to the north in the direction of Salem. Bonfires blaze and glowing sparks and cinders shoot high into the night sky as ecstatic revelers dance, chant, and perform archaic rites in dark ravines beyond where a mysterious white altar stone tops Meadow Hill. The midnight hour rapidly approaches. Soon the gateway to the land of the dead will open up where the Witch House once was.

What makes me so certain the dead will walk again? What is it about those prophetic words—"That is not dead which can eternal lie"—a mad Arabic poet coupled millennia ago in *Al Azif* that makes me such a firm believer in life after death?

Is it only a vain hope, a fevered dream or delirium, that I shall see my beloved alive again tonight?

Winds from the nearby salt ocean assault my olfactory senses with a flood of fetid fish odors, as if millions of dead and bloated cod suddenly float to the surface of the sea. The terrible stench makes me lightheaded and nauseous. I feel faint. I daren't faint and lose track of time.

I stumble from the bridge over the Miskatonic, hastening in the direction of the litter-filled vacant lot where the multi-angled old Witch House once stood. The tom-toms beat louder now, more frantic, more orgasmic. The tempo of archaic-sounding chants increases exponentially as certain strange words—words I've only read about in my researches but here-tofor never heard pronounced—are repeated over and over again. It's almost midnight. I sense subtle changes already occurring in the aether. The day of the dead is nearly upon us.

"Ia! Ia! Cthulhu fhtagn!" shout the revelers.

"Ia! Ia! Yog-Sothoth! Hail the gatekeeper, possessor of the silver key! The hour grows late."

"Open the gate! Open the gate! Open the gate."

"Open the gates of time and space. Show your face! Show your face."

"This is the date. This is the place."

"Open the gate and show your face!"

Violent winds send leaves and litter flying every which way, momentarily obscuring my vision. It's as if some conscious malignity seeks to hide what is about to happen from prying mortal eyes. But I'm nearly there. I cannot—will not—stop now. I stagger blindly forward, fighting against the mighty force of the gale-like wind with an equal intensity of my own.

I stagger and fall multiple times. Each time I hit the ground, I pick myself up and forge onward again until, at last, I achieve what seems to be the eye of the storm. A preternatural calm descends over all things and I'm finally able to see clearly.

The first thing I see: a spectral violet glow that dances, like a drunken will-o-wisp in concert with the beat of the tom-toms, materializing in the precise center of the century-vacant lot. The glow begins to spread out, first vertically, then horizontally, until it attains the approximate shape and size of a strangely-angled, multi-storied and multi-gabled, seventeenth-century abode.

The old Witch House of Keziah Mason lives again in Arkham, Massachusetts.

Within that glowing and still expanding violet mist, shifting shadows ofttimes appear entirely grotesque and sometimes almost humanoid, as if whatever spectral creatures exist inside are now material enough to cast dark silhouettes whenever they pass between lit lamps and thin draperies masking non-existent windows.

I edge closer in a vain attempt to peer inside the mist, but my vision can't penetrate the spectral veil. Is any of this real? Or is it only an illusion, a mad hallucination born of an irrational hope? Does my desire to once again behold the face of my dead wife cloud my vision and afflict my mind?

If it's real, should I be afraid? Is this truly the house of the dead materializing in front of my awestruck eyes? I may be foolish, but I am not a coward. I do not fear the dead.

"Laura!" I call out in desperation. "Come to me, my beloved! Please, Laura. Come to me."

Because I consider Laura and myself soul-mates forever—I have it in my head that we'll naturally be drawn together like two magnets of equal but opposite polarities—it never occurs to me she won't be the first or the only person who hears my call in the land of the dead. What fools these mortals be, especially when they're madly in love!

For what crawls out of that violet mist is not human, nor has it ever been. Grotesque beyond imagining, blasphemous and abominable, my horrified human eyes cannot begin to fathom an earthly purpose to its shape. It slides across the threshold between worlds like slime dripping from a decomposing corpse, solid one moment, liquid the next. The smell is so fetid that fish odors from before seem like the finest French perfume.

I hear slurping and squishing sounds as it advances toward me, exuding ectoplasmic pseudopods and multiple eyes affixed to two-foot-long tentacle-like stalks that protrude from the ambulating slime.

I watch as those multiple eyes all turn in unison to focus directly on me.

And sliding behind the first monstrosity, following so closely it's impossible to tell where one ends and another begins, comes an endless flow of putrid slime that reminds me first of afterbirth, then the overflow from a stuffed-up commode. As it exits the violet glow of the gateway, its true color is revealed as amphibian-green and not blood-red or excrement-brown as I originally thought.

I take a step back in total revulsion as the slime slowly advances toward me like sea-tides at full moon, and I'm suddenly filled with a primitive dread at beholding things that shouldn't exist but do. There can be no doubt that those *things*—whatever they may be—are not only alive but conscious that I'm watching them!

Are they coming for me? Do they wish to do me harm?

For the briefest moment I wonder if somehow, inadvertently, I'd summoned them out of the abyss when I called for Laura. Surely, these things are spawn of the devil or, at the very least, spawn of demons. My rational scientific mind reminds me that devils and demons are not real, but my eyes inform me otherwise.

These bubbling protoplasmic horrors prove as adaptive as undifferentiated stem cells, able to change their shape and function to whatever their environment presently requires. They propel themselves faster and faster as their pseudopods metamorph into true legs—not two or four legs like earth beings, but eight legs like Odin's fabled horse Sleipnir—and I turn and flee as if the devil himself pursues me.

That same mad Arab who penned the dreaded Necronomicon warned of similar entities he called shoggoths, created by the Great Old Ones to be their servants, which were not native to this earth. Shoggoths were bred to be infinitely adaptive, to mold themselves into perfect imitations of all forms, organs, and processes decreed by the telepathic hypnotic suggestions of their masters. They were not mindless creatures but intelligent beings who mocked their creators by mimicking their features and even their voices. Millions of years ago, the shoggoths rebelled against the Great Old Ones and took control of their domains.

Then they either fled the earth or disappeared beneath the sea.

Have they now returned as primal sludge?

Overhead, the gray and brown round-headed nightjars incessantly crow, "whup-a-rill, whup-a-ree. Whup-a-rill, whup-a-rheeeee!" Behind me, I hear, "Tekeli-li! Tekeli-li!"

Is there no place to run, nowhere to hide? I pound on the locked doors of three neighborhood houses, but none of the doors open to admit me at midnight on All-Hallow's Eve. I guess I can't blame the residents of Arkham. Who in their right mind would open their door to a stranger at this hour because who in their right mind would be knocking at this hour?

I chance a glance over my left shoulder and notice the amorphous forms are gaining on me, their four forward legs and four rearward legs as perfectly coordinated as the massive spinning tires of a diesel-driven eighteen-wheeler. Now out of range of the violet-colored mist, they glow an eerie phosphorescent green not unlike certain species of bioluminescent deep-sea creatures. Even as they continue resolutely toward me, they're continually changing, growing, developing, *becoming*.

Almost to the long bridge over the Miskatonic River, I have little hope of escaping the horror nearly upon me. If I can't outrun it and cannot hide from it, what else can I do?

I mount the bridge, fully expecting the unholy beasts to pounce before I achieve the east bank. But the terrible odor that has plagued me since midnight abruptly diminishes, and I am once again aware of the mile after mile of dead cod floating in the salt bay. Did the winds suddenly change direction from west to east because it's time for the gateway between worlds to close for another year?

As I cautiously peer behind me, I see the last of the not-yet fully-formed shoggoths scamper down the west bank on all eight legs to sink into the murky waters of the Miskatonic. The river momentarily glows with a green phosphorescence before the light disappears in the direction of the sea.

To what god or gods do I owe this amazing good fortune?

Without certain death hounding my backside, I'm able to think rationally and scientifically once more. Wasn't it in the dread Necronomicon I read shoggoths were bred to mature under water, distilling essential nutrients from the sea? Did they need to be submerged in water for the next phase of their development to occur?

If so, then the call of the sea had distracted the shoggoths from their prey.

I collapse onto the bridge and take the first deep breath I've been free to draw since before midnight. It's now after two. How could I have so easily lost track of time?

Less than five hours before daybreak. Although Laura won't be here with me to see the dawn, I'm grateful to be alive myself.

Thinking of Laura, I can visualize her face as last I saw her when she was yet alive. She gave me a sack lunch she had prepared for me to eat at the airport prior to departure. We kissed goodbye, and then I was off to far-away lands. She died in an automobile accident just days before I was scheduled to return.

"Laura, my love," I whisper to the image in my mind. "I'd give anything to hold you once more, to feel your sweet lips pressed to mine."

Then, amazingly, I see her, dressed exactly as I had seen her last. She steps from the waters of the Miskatonic and ascends the muddy bank to walk onto the bridge.

I stare at her in disbelief as she smiles and beckons to me. While I was running from the shoggoths, Laura must have answered my plaintive call heard in the land of the dead, crossed the threshold, and followed me here.

"Laura!" I shout in jubilation. "Laura, you're alive!"

I get to my feet, and I'm about to rush to her and gather her into my arms when I smell that same putrid stench of decomposition which overwhelmed me when the first shoggoth slid like afterbirth from the womb of the Witch House.

"Laura," I shout across the span of the bridge, "is it really you? Say something. If it's truly you, tell me you love me."

I see her lips move, but I cannot hear her answer.

"Laura," I say again. "Tell me you love me."

And then her baby blue eyes turn a hideous phosphorescent green as her luscious red lips form not the "I love you" I yearn to hear, but the mimicked "Tekeli-li" of the metamorphic shoggoths.

This time I don't hesitate. I spin around and take off running at top speed.

I ran and ran until I reached the Miskatonic University library. which remains open 24/7, including Christmas and Halloween.

I've no idea what happened to the shoggoths. I can only speculate they followed the Miskatonic to the sea. Personally, I don't care.

The Necronomicon claims shoggoths are as much at home in the deepest parts of the ocean as they are on dry land. They can live among the stars and thrive in the cold vacuum of outer space. They are omnivorous, but their greatest delicacy is said to be the consumption of entire human heads, especially brains and eyeballs. Shoggoths may have been the inspiration for the urban legend that zombies eat brains.

Now you know all that happened to me on the night of October 31st and the early morn of November 1st. I tried to relate these events as accurately as possible and in terms you could easily understand. I do have two earned doctorates from the University of Chicago, you know. I assure you, I'm a reputable scientist.

But I'm not certain even I can understand what dreadful things occurred in Arkham. Were the shoggoths able to read my mind? Is that how one of them knew to fashion itself into Laura to lure me into its clutches?

Although I do still believe in life after death and hope someday to be reunited with my beloved Laura, I now also believe in boogeymen and demons.

Why are you looking at me like that? You don't believe me? I swear it's true. Every word of it.

I assure you I am not insane. Do I look insane? Do I sound insane?

I'm not insane, I tell you. I'm not…

Ronnie and the River
by Christian Riley

Ronnie stood with easel on the back porch, studying the distant river. At the bottom of a shallow slope this water feature winded its way, a way that was less crooked in shape, but more decisive in manner, more matter of fact. An observer might suggest that this was an obstinate river, that it lacked purpose, save for that of reaching its destination by any means necessary. It was characteristically stark, hemmed only by dead, earthly-toned grass, no trees. There was nothing remarkable standing along its borders drinking from its great vein of nutrients. Truly, a different observer might also decide that this river was overwhelmingly useless, ugly and dumb, and almost certainly depressing to look at.

Blinking, Ronnie wondered vaguely where this river went. Then he recognized it for what it was at this exact moment: a bold contrast to the bright, turquoise sky he'd painted across the top half of his canvas. The palette in his hand began to shake, prompting him to exchange it for the Mountain Dew resting on the porch railing. He took a drink, set the can down, then scratched his fingers and wrists. Before he retrieved the palette, Ronnie looked again at the river, the sky, and then finally, at his painting. And it was here, at this moment, when he recognized that the *real* sky, above and beyond the river, also stood in contrast to what he'd painted. The real sky, in fact, was nowhere near blue. It was a violent conglomeration of deep purple and gray, with a blood-red sun half-buried into a pocket on the horizon.

Undeterred, Ronnie picked up his brush and smudged a dazzling yellow orb at the corner of his canvas, with bright rays that shone down onto the river, reflecting miracles of the imagination. A bird (or was it a bat?) suddenly flew past the porch, and Ronnie smiled happily—his dumb, enormously wide, mysteriously contagious, toothy grin.

Moments later, a beat-up Ford Ranger lurched along the side of the house. It came to a sputtering stop in the graveled lot behind the back porch. A thick-built man with long black hair staggered clumsily out, hugging grocery bags. He closed the door with a swing from his hip, then looked over and made eye-contact, smiled at Ronnie.

At once, Ronnie's face went cripple, leaving his mouth slack, a cave entrance for many a flying insect. He stared at the man, whom he knew as

Rick, Rick who rented the room above Ronnie's.

Rick grunted something to the effect of *Howdy*, then looked down and shuffled across the parking lot, up the back stairs. At this moment, a person might observe Rick and say that the man looked fatigued. Spent from his day of wrenching nuts and bolts, tooling with wheeled, combustible blocks of steel; a man with greased knuckles and hunched shoulders. Ronnie said nothing of the kind, of course, only stared vacantly, open-mouthed.

Rick climbed the stairs and emitted a faint chuckle. "Catching flies, are ya?" he said. Then he looked at Ronnie's painting, head tilted like a mutt's. His face screwed sideways; he glanced toward the horizon, then looked back at the canvas. Rick chuckled again, louder this time, then said, "Fucking retard. Are you color blind, also?"

Later that night, and by the light of a single lamp, Ronnie read a comic book. He was in a chair, a tired-looking Lazy Boy, the second of only two chairs in his entire dwelling. His home was all of a hundred and fifty square feet, a single room on the bottom corner of an old Victorian. The room had been renovated, half-heartedly, and accommodated for, legally, providing a bathroom and kitchenette. Ronnie wondered if the other rooms in the house were like his. Going on ten years now, and still he had no clue. He knew some of his neighbors, the other tenants, knew them by name, at least. But mostly these people kept to their selves, each of them buried amongst a host of troubles. At least once a week the police came by, affording these people with more of these troubles.

Rick, he was different, only in the manner of correspondence. The man indulged himself, so it seemed, in the way that he interacted with Ronnie, much to Ronnie's despair.

Like now, for example; Ronnie suspected that he would soon encounter another one of these interactions from his neighbor. He could sense it in the air: a buzzing vibration emanating from the walls. A leak of sorts—a *sewer* leak, draining from above. The dead silence…that was the suspicious part. The silence kept Ronnie on edge, was the calm before the storm, so-to-speak. Was this feeling of impending provocation simply Ronnie's imagination? Or was it the conditional byproduct of classical, behavior modification?

The answer to the riddle was short in coming. Before Ronnie finished his comic book, he'd heard the sounds incumbent to the concoction of one of Rick's interactions: the arrival of another man, a buddy of his; their loud guffaws; the certain involvement of libations; and then, sometime later, the subsequent poundings on the floor, which was, of course, Ronnie's ceiling. He figured they were wrestling but, like always, these noises ended up with both men laughing voraciously, and then screaming, "He's a retard!" The words always seemed to hit right in Ronnie's ear, as if they'd pressed their mouths into the floor to better effect the distance of their hollering.

* * * *

Work was Ronnie's reprieve. Work was his salvation from the annoyances of his life, as it was simple and mundane work, and could be described by an observer as being entirely lonesome—a quality which never seemed to weigh Ronnie down. Indeed, he loved his job. A low-paying janitorial position at the local university, it kept Ronnie busy, yet afforded him time to ponder, which he liked. He also worked late hours, a shift that began in the early evening, and went well into the night—hence the absence of others.

The university itself was ancient of time, with halls and rooms and courtyards having witnessed the passing of several generations of students. Such a student could observe smooth, oak columns; rustic, iron-wrought fences; aged paintings; and dark, walnut-clad walls. Reliefs, depicting great battles between man and indescribable beasts, embellished full balustrades. Certain ceilings had been styled with great murals, scenes from a pre-biblical time, perhaps, according to the pagan-like themes portrayed. And finally, straight through the university grounds drifted the same river that passed by Ronnie's home, adding a sense of convenient familiarity for the janitor.

Gothic and nightmarish in quality, the university's atmosphere was sorely wasted on Ronnie, who, of no fault of his own, was incapable of great leaps of the imagination. Indeed, as he dusted surfaces and swept floors late into the night, Ronnie's mind never once taunted him with the paranormal dreams one would expect to come from such a place. Mostly, he thought about his comic books, or his paintings, and sometimes, with a hint of dread, he thought about Rick. Furthermore, there was an uncanny resolve to Ronnie's dismissive aspect, which begged a unique form of attention. And, if distantly observed by another person—a person *with* a notable imagination—as Ronnie mopped floors, or emptied trash bins, it would seem that while in the quiet solitude of the night, the university as a whole also studied Ronnie.

And so it was, on one of these enigmatic nights, that Ronnie was presented with a piece of campus long forgotten.

It happened in the library, while Ronnie was dusting the bookcases. A book fell from off the shelf (was this Ronnie's fault?), and when he reached down to pick it up, he noticed a crease in the far corner of the floor, from under the antique rug. Curious, he pulled the corner of the rug up and discovered a small, wooden door. An ancient door. A secret door, apparently. Ronnie tested it, and found that the door was unlocked. It opened with an aged, grinding wail, a metal-on-metal sound. A dank odor emerged from the depths, a cold breeze sweeping across Ronnie's face. There was an iron ladder just below the opening, dropping quickly into dark shadow. With a shrug, Ronnie grabbed the first rung and climbed down.

* * * *

He'd painted a small boat on the river. Just a dinghy, large enough for a person to sit in. Ronnie planned, in fact, to illustrate himself inside this same boat, but someone beat him to it.

Largely, it was Ronnie's fault, for leaving his work-in-progress on the easel, and on the back porch. When he rode his bike home from work, past blinking street lamps, through darkened alleys, and even, at certain spots, alongside the river, Ronnie imagined in full detail just how he would illustrate his self in the boat—down to the smallest shadow. However, when he arrived at home, he found that someone had crudely formed, in black paint, a stick-figure standing in the boat. The cartoonish character sported a wide grin, not unlike Ronnie's, and was grasping an exceedingly large penis, (along with a pair of hairy balls), from which spurted into the river orbicular gobbets.

Largely, it *was* Ronnie's fault. He should have known better. Should've stashed his easel into his room before he left for work. He did this now, and he sulked in his Lazy-Boy afterward, listening with a brooding aspect at what he swore was Rick, snickering from up above. The next morning, as Ronnie stepped outside for a walk, he discovered this same neighbor sitting on the front steps, smoking a cigarette. And the man's subsequent response dispelled any reservations Ronnie might have entertained the night before.

"Hey, Ronnie-boy," Rick said, "is it true—that retards have big dicks?" He followed his words with a gleeful cackle, then stared as Ronnie walked quietly away.

* * * *

On his third night after discovering the secret door in the library, Ronnie began to see strange hieroglyphs. Oddly enough, he saw these symbols amongst everyday patterns, embedded in curves and lines, adjoining or bisecting complex forms of matter. At the conjunction of a computer and a desk, he saw a hieroglyph. In the folds of a hanging coat, he saw another. Then, in the river, on his way to work, amongst the gently lapping ripples…full paragraphs.

Ronnie had no clue what these symbols meant, and was only vaguely aware of their presence. And he certainly did not suspect that the discovery of these symbols, in due time, would have an impact on him.

A few nights later, after returning home from work, Ronnie ran into Rick once again. Caught the man red-handed, in fact, shitting in a box placed in front of Ronnie's door. After realizing his bust, Rick stood erect and ran for the stairs, laughing maliciously as he worked up his pants.

More of the same, Ronnie thought, with a shake of his head. He picked up the box of shit, gingerly, and placed it outside near the dumpster. On his way back inside, he inadvertently glanced at the river, and then froze. Under a pale moon Ronnie read the glyphs riding the current, and this time he knew what they meant. This time, he could read them.

* * * *

Two more days passed, finding Ronnie once again running into Rick on the back porch. Ronnie was almost finished with painting away the crude figure in the boat, when Rick walked outside.

"Aww, man, you erased it," Rick complained. He had a cigarette in his mouth, was spinning a keychain around his finger. "What the fuck for?"

Ronnie remained silent. He shifted his feet, fidgeted with his palette, all the while staring blankly at Rick.

"Well, say something, stupid retard. Why'd you go and erase it?"

More long seconds passed. Rick turned, was about to walk away, then Ronnie said, "I'm not a retard."

Rick turned and faced him. "Say what?"

"I'm not a retard," Ronnie repeated. "I have Down's syndrome."

At this, Rick grinned. "Same difference, ain't it? You're still a dumb fuck." Then he turned and walked down the steps, got in his truck and drove away.

When the dust settled, and the silence of seclusion mounted the porch once again, Ronnie's stare found that of the river beyond. He observed the ripples glisten against the morning light; and he read each and every hieroglyph along that same stretch of water. He read them out loud, like poetry, and he used a precise inflection and beat, and he heard himself speak in a tongue that defied reason. And then, after reading the last of the symbols, Ronnie casually lifted his palette and went back to painting.

* * * *

He was in the bathroom getting ready for work when he heard the men laughing outside. It was a late, Friday afternoon, and apparently Rick had gotten off work early. He and a friend were in the parking lot behind the house, up to no good, Ronnie presumed. He tried to rack his mind around what it could be, assuming some form of mischief was in process, and also, assuming the target of such trouble was indeed, him. Eventually, Ronnie left his room, and this was when he discovered the nature of Rick's delight.

Ronnie kept his bike chained up outside, under the back porch, where, incidentally, Rick and a friend were now sitting, drinking beers. They were both suspiciously quiet, and obvious in their manner of repressing laughter. But they gave up the struggle and roared triumphantly, once Ronnie found the state in which his bike was in.

It was a deer, he realized. Road kill, most likely. The carcass had been grotesquely splayed open, roughly applied upon, and interwoven, into the frame and spokes of Ronnie's bicycle. Entrails draped raggedly over the handlebars, and the seat was covered with something black and sticky, which Ronnie assumed was blood. If it wasn't for the head, (creatively positioned onto the handlebar frame, as if to stare pensively at the bicycle rider), Ronnie would have had no clue what kind of creature it was.

It took him almost an hour to clean the animal off his bike, with Rick and his friend laughing, making crude comments the whole time. Ronnie ignored them, up until he at last sat on his bike, and prepared to leave. He looked stiffly at the men, and they stared back, a humorous, inquisitive gleam in their eyes. At that moment, Ronnie saw, and *heard* the hieroglyphs, and then he stated in a most uncharacteristic way, "The One of Infinite Disorder, Lecher of the Foul Water, shall seek revenge upon your kind."

Both Rick and his friend appeared dumbfounded. They stared at Ronnie, confusion and humor battling across their faces. Finally, Rick replied with, "What the hell did you say?" And then he laughed, along with his friend, as they watched Ronnie quietly ride away.

As soon as Ronnie arrived at work, he wasted no time. Immediately, he went to the hidden door in the library and climbed down.

* * * *

When the last day came, Ronnie was on the porch, adding the final touches to his painting. It was a Saturday morning—a cold and gloomy morning, with rain clouds that sat low and heavy in the sky. Ronnie had been up for most of the night, unable to sleep, all because of Rick and his friend, and their drunken commotion gushing down from above. Every few minutes they'd screamed something about Ronnie, about him being a retard, or about the size of his penis, and how he liked to fuck dead animals. On and on and on, their clamor went…while on and on, Ronnie whispered a strange language into the night.

They were still asleep now, Ronnie was sure. He wondered if they'd wake when the darkness came, or if they'd sleep right through it.

The final touches to Ronnie's painting included him standing in the river, facing the boat he'd painted earlier. Also, he added a black streak in the sky, at the horizon—a distant cloud, perhaps…or, perhaps something else. When he was finished, Ronnie set his brush and palette on the railing, and stepped back. He studied the painting for a minute, nodding with approval. Then he picked up his brush, dabbed it copiously in black paint, and stroked a single, massive hieroglyph across the entire scene.

In the minutes that followed, Ronnie found himself walking through dead grass, and toward the river. He heard the deep resonance the sky made as it split open, but he missed the long shadows falling behind him. The water was warmer than Ronnie expected, and he met it up to his knees before the dinghy reached his fingers. Carefully, he climbed in, and carefully, he took a seat. The boat set slowly adrift, and Ronnie watched as the current pushed him along, toward a vague, yet indisputable destination. He smiled, and then let one hand slip into the water, felt its tepid touch.

From afar, an observer might suggest that this man in the boat contained a sheepish quality. That his grinning stare pushed toward the boundaries of the horizon with an expecting, yet flat gaze; as if, despite his excitement, he had all the time in the world to wait.

Still, a different observer might relinquish this observation altogether, in lieu of the other, more dramatic scene, unfolding in the background. Indeed, this second witness would likely gasp in undeniable horror as he watched the colossal appendage reach down from the sky, crash through a gabled roof, and then pluck the shrieking bodies into a black and terrifying end.

And finally, it is quite possible that a third observer, perhaps that of a bird, or a bat in flight, may observe the fallen painting now left abandoned in a gravel parking lot—a painting depicting that of a yellow sun with a turquoise sky, and a world of paradise as seen along the shores of a thriving river.

Cellar Dweller
by Franklyn Searight

Alan remembered his early days with clarity as he sat back in the lounge chair, swiveling shards of shivering ice in his mouth and watching clouds floating above the peaceful lake to where he and his wife, Sheila, had retired. It amused him to see their resemblance to beings he had bested in the past.

As a former reporter for the Arkham Daily News, he had spent a good part of his life investigating and writing about strange and dark corners of the country, places unknown to average Americans. He was seldom surprised to find legends were often based on solid, though perhaps slightly exaggerated, fact.

In his infancy, Alan had shown no sign of one day being the intrepid nemesis of the Elder Gods who had arrived on Earth countless millions of years ago. It was not until his early teen years he learned of his heritage, which included being the great, great, etcetera, grandson of the infamous sorcerer of the burning sands of Yemen, known as Abdul Alhazred, the Mad Arab of Ciené, and author of the *Kitab al-Azif.*

It was an ominous legacy for a youngster to inherit which would follow him throughout his life. As a baby, it manifested itself almost right away, even though he was not yet the fearless, resourceful oppressor of the Elders with sharpened instincts to combat and withstand their nefarious attempts to return to Earth and deal with its denizens as they wished. Growing up in the small Massachusetts town of Arkham he was not immune to their threats.

For the most part, he was a happy, enthusiastic American lad, with no especial talents beyond those of his little friends, yet with the potential to rise above formidable obstacles threatening to complicate the direction his life would take as he overcame fears others did not encounter.

The differences were subtle. His fledgling playmates, for instance, did not feel at all uneasy when near their cellar doors, as Alan did. He was too small and immature to understand why or even acknowledge his instinctive fears of the unknown. Since the earliest days he could recall, he knew this was so. During those times when the door was accidentally left open, allowing him to see the darkness welling up from the basement, his uneasiness became so intense he would turn his head to avoid seeing something monstrous plodding up the steps.

Of course, nothing did, but he still expected the very worst to materialize.

His parents, Roland and Sarah Hasrad, an easy-going and understanding couple, knew of the little tyke's aversion to the depths below, but never comprehended his dislike of them.

He remembered, long into his dotage, the one time he was taken by his mother down the gloomy steps to the basement pantry for a jar of strawberry preserves, and his reaction convincing him to never descend the steps again. He had been near the bottom when he began to sweat profusely and his heart raced as his face broke out in unbecoming blotches. The descent completed, his words became slurred, his steps faltered, and his eyes seemed to dance awkwardly in their sockets. Alan had bolted away, rushed back up the steps to the kitchen and from there to the sanctuary of his bedroom where he trembled, his face drained of blood and blanched a ghastly, ghostly white. There he remained for several hours enveloped in the solace and peace it offered, eventually playing with a set of toy soldiers he had received for Christmas.

When asked what he had seen or heard, he shook his head and innocently said, "Someting' down there," and would not, or could not, elaborate upon the simple statement.

"It's characteristic of a growing intellect," Mom and Dad reasoned, certain he would eventually grow out of it. Sensitive to his unusual aversion, they refrained from assigning to him chores that would take him into the lower level, even when the lights were on, wary of the fuss he would likely make and the excuses he would offer for what he believed to be an extremely good reason.

Never again was he asked to make the scary descent into the depths below.

As the years progressed, and he graduated from the immaturity of puberty to adolescence, and from there to a gawky teenager, one would think his anxieties would lesson—but such was not the case. Being a rational individual, he knew there was nothing for him to fear from down below. His parents, when occasion required it, would open the door and descend, thinking nothing of it. His mother would return with a few potatoes stored down in the coolness, or Father might return with a Phillips Head screwdriver from his tool bench. Both would retrieve whatever was stored below when needed, and feel no degree of trepidation whatsoever.

But not Alan. In all other respects, he was a fearless, normal youth, able to scramble with ease around the scaffolding of a building being constructed, or quickly dispatch a blocker protecting the quarterback of an opposing team, or climb the tallest tree in the neighborhood. No problem whatsoever.

'One day, in his mid-teens, he had been forced by armed burglars into the cellar where he sat, out of their way, leaving them to loot the home without fear of interference. Alan had objected, but their weapons, being quite persuasive, decided the issue. The door was locked behind him, and it was not until three hours later his parents returned home. They found him on the top step behind the locked door, curled into a ball of fear. He was trembling and whimpering, drenched in perspiration and incoherent, refusing to tell anyone what had frightened him so badly.

The truth was, he had blacked out almost immediately, only regaining his senses from time to time, so petrified he was afraid to twitch a muscle. He had no idea what monstrous being might be nearby, and for years ascribed his fear as a normal characteristic of growing youth.

His unrealistic dread increased the older he grew, and by the age of seventeen, he was still unable to conquer his aversion to the cellar, something that would always bother him. Still, he knew with certainty there *was* something down there—he just did not know what, not until the day came when he decided to challenge his qualms and determine just what it was.

He had recently celebrated another birthday when, sitting at the dining room table with his parents one evening, he felt the urge to share with them a recent thought.

"You know," he said, hesitantly, "you've been living here for the last twenty-six years, and me for seventeen—all my life."

"Yes?" said his mother, spearing a green bean on her plate.

"Well, I was thinking: That's a long time. Stats tell us most people live in the same place for about six years and then move on."

"So?" said his father, looking up from the table. "Sounds like a statistic you made up yourself."

"Maybe it does, but haven't you ever felt the urge to move away?"

"Why would we want to do that?" asked Mom, her mouth full and chewing slowly.

"Yeah," said Dad, "my job's nearby, and my friends and relations not far away. Why would we want to leave our home-sweet-home?"

"I didn't mean *far* away. Even a few blocks would be nice. New homes are being built over by Hangman's Hill you might like."

"They might be overly expensive, too, you know, and our home is paid for. Did you think of that?"

"Well, no, but you have a good job. New surroundings are always nice."

"Says you. We should be content with what we have: nice house, well built, sturdy and comfortable; plenty of good, nourishing grub in the kitchen. We've been quite happy living here, you know?"

"Yeah, I know…but still…"

"Hey, just a minute; now I get it," his father said, allowing his fork to slip to his plate. "You want to live somewhere else because of this cellar obsession you have. Right!"

"Wrong. Well, that might be a little part of it," Alan admitted. "But aside from that, it would be pleasant to live in new surroundings; different school, new friends. It's an old house, remember, and built before the nineteen hundreds."

"Don't you have lots of friends, right here?"

"Yeah, I guess so."

"You'll be leaving next year for four years of college, anyway."

"I guess so," he admitted, adding, in an unheard undertone, "but I'd leave this very minute if I could."

"Given any thought to a career for yourself?" asked Dad, changing the subject, forestalling further argument his son might make about relocating.

Alan sighed and sipped from his water glass. He would never be able to convince them to move, and would just have to endure the coming days until his collegiate career began. After that, he silently vowed, he would not return unless absolutely necessary.

"Well, you've known for years I've had this fascination for studying words and their entomologies, and so on, and also working as an investigative reporter, maybe for the *Arkham Daily News* or one of its competitors. I'll probably be doing most of my collegiate work at the Miskatonic University, right here in Arkham. It's not far away, so I can commute every day and live here instead of a dormitory."

"That'll go easy on my wallet, Son."

"I think it's a wonderful idea," encouraged Mom.

"And then I'll do post graduate work somewhere else, maybe Saudi Arabia or Iran."

"Some other country? Why would you want to do that?" Mother wondered.

"Because it's a part of the world I find greatly interesting, and possibly because of our ancestry. Somehow, I'm extremely attracted to it. Dad, you've mentioned from time to time the name of Abdul Alhazred, and that's where he lived, the mad poet of Sanaá in Yemen. He lived in Damascus during the 8th century."

Father added, "I'd like to know a little more about him, also. After all, he is one of our distant ancestors."

"Yeah, and he did dabble in esoteric matters you once told me, said he talked of foreign gods and goddesses and entities drifting down from the stars to settle for a time here on earth. I have an urge to flesh out these stories, to find out more about the fantastic creatures subjugating our planet, and learn about their minions who are present to this day involved in bringing about their return.

"Surely, Alan, you know that's utter nonsense," Mom interjected. "Pure hokum."

"Is it? I don't know, and I'd like to find out just what the situation really is. A normal job wouldn't provide me with the opportunity. So...as I do have an ability with the use of words, it occurs to me a journalistic career might be my calling and an investigative reporter would provide me with the ideal opportunities."

"Utter nonsense," said the father voicing his opinion once again, agreeing with his wife's skepticism.

"Now, don't discourage him, Roland. It's the lad's life and he knows how he wants to live it."

Over the years, attempts to conquer his fear of the spooky depths diminished, except for one time when he was twenty years old and on holiday from classes at Miskatonic University. He had read a story, assigned by his teacher, about a young man who accepted a dare to spend the night in a reputedly haunted house. He knew it was a fictional yarn, but was able to identify with the young hero and understand how traumatizing it would be if real, and how similar the situation was to his own. It emboldened him to face whatever lived within the shadows below his house. How would he feel, he wondered, if he had to spend the *entire night* in the expansive region below? The hero of the tale had left the next day, unscathed, undaunted, and ready to face the world with nerves intact. Could he, Alan, do the same?

One evening soon afterward the right conditions fell into place. His parents were gone for the evening to see the latest movie. He was feeling extremely confident as he descended into the basement, carrying with him cushions from the chaise lounge, a pillow and blankets, and a large, family-sized bag of chips. Among his other accumulation, he remembered to bring with him his transistor radio and the novel he was currently reading.

At the last moment, Alan slipped into his pocket a stone amulet upon which had been engraved the Elder Sign, an icon offering protection against evil forces, a powerful weapon able to banish servants of Cthulhu and the Outer Gods about which he had been learning. Perhaps it would be of use.

He was prepared to tough it out.

If necessary, he could easily climb back up the steps and out of the cellar again. He was no longer a little boy with the fears of one, but a large, stalwart youth with the ability to take care of himself. If he was unable to fall asleep right away, the radio would provide social communication for him.

He had not finished the first chapter of his book when his radio suddenly stopped emitting any sound, and this surprised him as he knew a fresh battery had been inserted.

He looked up and over, his gaze settling first upon his father's workbench, and then over to the cement lid covering the sewer line from where a humming noise seemed to emanate. Out from it was drifting a fine haze corkscrewing toward the ceiling. Alan lowered his book, the page where he left off unmarked, and moments later his radio dropped to the concrete flooring. Listlessly, he stared in perplexity at the spiraling vapor which he suspected was a combination of odious sewer gasses creating the phenomenon.

"I must have been sleeping," he theorized out loud, "dreaming without realizing it."

One of his teachers had been reading to the class just the other day "Pickman's Model", written by a prominent author of eighty years ago. The parallel of what had been written then and his situation now was not exact, and yet was strangely similar. In the story, a ghoul had emerged from depths far below an artist's residence to act as a model.

Alan's eyes were attracted to the circular rim of concrete in the corner. He had noticed it when forced into the basement against his will, but had paid no attention to it at the time. But now he did and, not certain what it was, walked over and studied it more carefully, staring down at a five-pointed pentagram etched into its surface. Esoteric numbers and letters of Arabic, or another Middle Eastern configuration, were engraved upon the surface, reminding him of the protective charm he carried. This must be a part of the sewer system, he reasoned, but could think of no reason why the senseless eruditions were not written in the English language. It made no sense to him.

"Oh, well," he thought, his spirit of investigation and adventure controlling normally good judgment. "I'll take a peak down there and see what's to be seen, maybe discover what's making the vapor."

The lid was heavier than expected and not easily pushed aside as anticipated, but after assorted grunts and curses, it began to move far enough for him to peer downward into the darkness. The lone lightbulb in the ceiling above did not provide enough illumination to see very far along the brickwork, disappearing like a telescope into the depths, and he wondered just how far down the actual bottom was. Too bad he had not brought a flashlight allowing him to see all the way. The haze continued upward, no greater nor lesser than before, and touching it he found its texture to be the consistency of smoke.

He considered. In his pocket he had some change and from it selected a penny to toss into the pit and wait for it to strike bottom, giving him some idea of its depth. He waited and waited, expecting to hear a metallic clink, but nothing was heard and he concluded it must have landed on something soft, or kept going all the way to China. Rumors he had heard indicated unseen tunneling snaked and twisted below the streets of Arkham for miles and miles.

With nothing more to be learned, he prepared to return to the little recess he had assembled and read more of his book. Attempting to move the lid back to where it had been, however, he discovered it was much heavier than anticipated, more difficult to shove forward than it had earlier been to pull back, as though something from below were dragging in the opposite direction he was pushing. The lid would simply not budge. Grumbling and cussing did no good this time, and he decided to leave it there until more of his strength returned. Before leaving the basement he would try again.

And then, unexpectedly, it began to slide more easily, revealing more and more of the curious shaft.

And something else.

He was not as astounded as others might have been. The haze, still creeping up from below, began to solidify and evolve into an indescribably ugly creature just as terrifying as the ghoulish models had been for Richard Pickman.

Whatever it was, it had the features of an elderly genie-like atrocity rising out of the drain like an image floating from a bottle. It began speaking to him, its bulbous torso encircled by folded arms as it glared at Alan with hostile intent. The young man inched his way backward, slowly, as a deep, sonorous voice began to speak and miasma continued spiraling upward.

When the *something* fully emerged, Alan was almost petrified.

"It's about time you came," it greeted him, annoyance curling its globular lips. "I've asked for you, called and called repeatedly," it claimed with the rapidity of a Tommy Gunn. "But you would not hear me; you would not come."

It was now a black and white, transparent vision filling in with an assorted coloration of the rainbow.

Alan ignored its absurd appearance and instead asked, when able to vocalize his thoughts, "Are you a genie or what? You sort of look like one."

"Believe me, I am, but more than that. I am your foulest nightmare," the revelation spoke. "Come closer."

"I'm fine where I am," was Alan's determined refusal.

"Come closer," the immensity directed him once again.

Alan refused to budge, and then did, not because he wanted to but his muscles moved against his will.

"I hunger," it intoned, rubbing its enormous belly.

It occurred to Alan, considering the size of its paunch, it had not been starving very long. He became stationary, not advancing the slightest of an inch. All would be well, he believed, as long as the outrage remained where it was. If it came closer, he feared he might scramble out of the cellar, up the steps, and conceal himself beneath his bed as he had done once before.

"Only you can save me, young Hasrad," it said in a monotone voice.

"Who...what...are you?" Alan fumbled.

"My name is Hudhayfah, young sir, former friend and ally of Abdul Alhazred, perhaps known to you as the Mad Arab of Sanaá?"

Alan gave no indication he did and eyed the frightful fiend expectantly.

"Abdul was your grandfather more than twelve hundred years ago."

"You knew him?" the youngster asked of the ogre-faced being. "If you did, you must be quite old, yourself."

"At least hundreds of years, I calculate. I was old when Abdul was a little boy. I lost track of my birthdate centuries ago, Boy. Heck, I not only knew him, I devoured him.

"One day, I was sent on a diplomatic mission, the jar in which I lived smuggled across two borders, and was given to Abdul as an inconsequential gift for an insignificant favor. He decided to keep me after learning I'm a mediocre conjuror, of sorts, who trafficked with the dark underworld.

"Our relationship was parasitic, he supplying my need for sustenance and protection, while I provided him with certain dark knowledge which had come down to me through vast ages. He carried me about in a Byzantine bottle, and we were happy to profit from the association we shared.

"In the eighth century we visited the ruins of Memphis and explored its subterranean depths. Later on, we spent ten years traveling about the Roba El Khaliyeh, the southern desert of Arabia. It was also my privilege to travel with him to Dreamland's Vale of Panath, which you likely know is inhabited and guarded by evil haunts. It was there I twice saved his accursed life.

"From me he learned many forbidden, outré secrets and wrote an infamous book of abysmal evil known as the dreaded *Kitab al-Azif*, later as the infamous *Necronomicon*, of which you must have heard."

Alan looked at the frightful fiend expectantly and shook his head innocently. "Not so."

"You must have, but I caution you, young sir, to never *read* it, especially during the hours of darkness."

"Abdul learned from you?"

"Yes, indeed, from me, Hudhayfah, within whose bosom resides the knowledge of the Old Ones who came to Earth millions of years ago to subjugate developing mankind."

"Hudhayfah, huh? A strange name I won't forget."

"You have no time to forget, little man," it answered. "I am your disaster. I ate your grandpapa on the streets of Damascus more than a thousand years ago."

"So, you're the one, are you?" Alan said accusingly, regaining composure while fingering the protective weapon concealed in his pocket, his grim lips pursed in determination. "I did hear rumors," he said reproachfully, "of something snatching him out of the air one day in Damascus and the treacherous feast in which you ate him in front of a gathering multitude of witnesses."

"You heard correctly, young sir. I am unique in my ability to vanish and appear at will, and did not want anyone to know of my presence until I was ready to grab him. Oh, he was good, alright."

"What possessed you to do such an awful thing?"

"He threatened to throw my bottle, with me inside, into the Crimean Sea. Now prepare to be eaten."

"Be warned, I'll battle you all the way down your vile gullet."

"Oh, ho, you would defy me, would you? I have not eaten in more than three hundred years and you deny me sustenance?" It slurped an enormous quantity of air and ballooned outward like a Thanksgiving Parade oddity nodding to the crowd, its expansiveness nearly filling the entire chamber.

"Emphatically, yes! How come you're here, anyway?" asked young Alan.

"A multitude of generations passed, when one of your Grand pappy's grandsons, a deceitful descendant named Hakeem, in whose care I was being guarded, captured me, shriveled me, and imprisoned me into a small capsule before dragging me across the bounding turbulence to America, cozy and secure in my bottle. Still not content, he imprisoned me here in this very cellar of the home he was building. Here I have languished ever since. I never sampled him, as I did your awful great…great…and so on… grandfather who's only positive quality was he was easy to catch—and was extremely tasty.

"When I complained to Hakeem my container was too confining for my bulk, the villain pitched me into the sewage system. When I reached the bottom, it smashed, releasing me into the slimy mess where I was free to roam about in its luxurious spaciousness. It became my home and here I have existed, safeguarded for you, Alan Hasrad, as a portion of your inheritance—you being the last of the Al-Hazred descendants."

"You lie or jest, deceitful one. Why would my kinsman bring you here?"

"Revenge, of course, for the manner in which Abdul treated him."

"I had nothing to do with your being here," Alan stated, "so why consume me? I can help you survive, provide you with nourishment you need to live.

"Anyway, I doubt if you even have teeth."

"Oh, don't I?" it returned, inflating itself more than before, filling the entire room except for Alan. It, whatever it was, opened its mouth, exposing bicuspids and tusks, incisors and fangs; a broken molar sat askew in the back of a blood-red maw.

"What think you of these choppers, miniature man? Impressive, eh? I must be fed! I thirst! I have been deprived of food and drink for many generations since eating the last Hazrad, he who betrayed me. Now I am free to remedy the omission."

"If you're really so famished," Alan offered. "I can provide you with sustenance from the grocery stores."

"But it's *your* blood and *your* flesh I must have before leaving this accursed place."

"I will never accommodate you," Alan informed it disagreeably, regaining composure and clutching the mystic icon unseen in his pocket. His grim lips pursed in determination, responding as forcefully as before. "Forget it, whoever or whatever you are."

"Hah! And now you've come along," said the other-world monster, stomping upon the barrier and pushing it aside. "I should be more appreciative, but more than anything else, I am starved."

"Too bad," asserted Alan. "You must dine elsewhere. There is a world out there upon which you can slack your thirst and fill your bursting belly. You must provide food and drink for yourself and trouble me no longer. I'm sure you won't falter in your quest for edibles."

"You are correct in your belief I will prosper, but I cannot accept your offer, mini man; you look much too tasty."

"You disappoint me, Hudhayfah, but before you mangle my bones do not forget you are a genie and owe me three wishes."

"I am *partially* jinn—true—but only on my mother's side and I owe you no wishes. You have released me and I am free to go."

"I see. You will not gratify me with a wish, but perhaps you will grant me a favor—a little one."

"And what would it be, little bloke? Yes, I might gift you a small one before I pick your skeleton and slack my thirst upon your vital fluids. Tell me this kindness you would have me do."

"My penny. I dropped it in the shaft to gauge how deep it was."

"And you want me to retrieve it, do you?" it said, pushing its proboscis closer to Alan's face. "For you, I will do it. It is a small thoughtfulness, easily done, and will take little time— although it's a sloppy and soggy mess down there and might take a while to find.

"Excuse me. I'll be back as soon as possible, and my feast will begin."

With those ominous words, the gruesomeness turned and dived without thinking into the sewer line, squeezing through the edges of the open shaft, the last of him disappearing out of sight like an accomplished high diver plunging into unknown depths to which he was accustomed.

"Damn!" thought Alan. "Damn! Damn! Damn! What in God's name have I done? I can't allow an inhuman being to get away from here and into the world. The dark ones only know what havoc and destruction it would cause."

Alan breathed a hearty sigh and wasted no time in darting to the shaft, believing the abomination was long on mass but short on brains. He shoved the lid over the hole with renewed strength, closing the opening. His subconscious must have taken over, permeating his muscles with adrenalin and whatever additives were necessary to equip him with super normal strength. He laid his talisman on the concrete lid, well aware of the mystical and paranormal powers it had to ward off the powers of evil, entrapping the monster once again.

Alan considered. Should he return to the reclining chair and lay down, perhaps to nap until the return of Hudhayfah, or pick up his book and begin reading again? No, he would only soon set it aside; there was little use in reading the same sentence over and over again. He might also pack up the items he brought with him and go upstairs to bed.

What he really preferred was to pursue his thoughts about Hudhayfah, to see where they led. He stared off into the distance then allowed his eyes to wonder downward, settling upon the covering slab, wondering if Hud had acknowledged its defeat like a good sport and accepted the coming years of forced imprisonment.

Suddenly, he heard noises of gigantic muscles working at the lid and held his breath as it raised nearly a sliver of an inch before settling back into place. Hudhayfah was back! Something quite weighty, some nebulous force was exerting itself to keep the enormous one imprisoned, holding it down,

From below came the surprised exclamation of a subterranean vocalization growing louder as the seconds passed.

"What are you doing, Alan?" it came, an eerie cry of desperation. "I have your penny! Release me and I will give it to you."

"Nothing doing," returned the lad, a broad smile expanding upon his face, growing wider as he heard more struggling sounds of the genie attempting to push the lid aside. They ceased after a few moments when the imprisoned grotesque realized it was having no effect.

"Forget it, treacherous one," advised Alan. "Do you really suppose I'd release you again?"

Alan's thoughts drifted over other challenges he had won during his

exhilarating career, pondering many years laced with some failures but more successes. Satisfied with his life's work, thus far, he wondered what, if any, adventures were destined to come his way.

Now in the prime of life, his hair thinning and turning from gray to burnished silver, Alan reflected upon the curious, extremely dangerous but meaningful life he led spending a good many years pursuing creatures wallowing in the dark crevices of the world.

"You seem so remote, so introspective, dear," said Sheila, coming from the house and arriving with a tray and glasses of iced tea. "A penny for your thoughts."

"That's all? A meager cent? I was thinking of Hudhayfah, a creature I knew many years ago—ugly as proverbial sin—wondering if it continues to exist confined in the twisting corridors beneath the streets of Arkham.

"Someday I'll tell you how a penny saved my life."

Yellow Labeled VHS Tape
by R.C. Mulhare

"Who hauls in all this junk? People that clean out hoarder houses and old people's attics?" Mason grumbled, as he trailed his Aunt Melanie down the main aisle of the Red Dot Flea Market, located in what had been a box factory on the outskirts of Leominister. The place resembled a row of stalls full of junk typical of most attics or basements: one consisted entirely of porcelain dolls, the shelves of another groaned with hardback bestsellers from the last fifty years, including what looked like the complete works of Stephen King. The next one was jammed with boxes of baseball cards, some still sealed in cellophane. Most of the sellers and buyers had put age forty well behind them, except for the babies and second-graders obviously out with Grandma.

"Trust me, Mason, I've found a lot of treasures here,"Aunt Melanie said. "A lot of the sellers don't know what they have on their hands, or they want to move it fast."

"How about they don't move the creepy dolls?" Mason said, looking away from a booth full of kitchen gadgets, FiestaWare and more porcelain dolls. He could just imagine the little darlings with the masks of innocence coming to life and finding creative uses for the orange peelers and egg slicers in the baskets below them.

"Yeah, there's always a lot of those," she said, approaching a large booth of furniture, mostly corner tables, standing desks, an armoire and a heavy carved-wood headboard that lacked a foot board.

"I don't wanna think about why they'd have so many of those," Mason said.

"You wanna keep browsing while I talk with Jake about that armoire?"

"Sure, anything to give those things some space," Mason said, moving on, dodging a woman in a purple sweatshirt and a red church hat with a purple sequined hat band, riding a purple scooter towing a tiny trailer full of shopping bags behind her.

He quick walked past a booth of shoddy-looking tools, and another full of fiber-optic silk flower arrangements and other fiber-optic doodahs.

Wall to wall VHS tapes filled the shelves of the next booth, mostly commercially taped movies and box sets of TV series, some easily available on DVD now and others hard to find, while the lower shelves held bootlegged movies on previously blank cassettes, titles hand-written on labels or the slipcases. In a corner, on the floor, he found a box of tapes shuffled together into a pile. Mason sorted through them, reading the labels: "The Telephone—Poulenc". "Hopfrog—Poe/DeJasu", "The Driving Lesson", "Titus Andronicus", "Ingrid's Monologues and one woman shows", and one with a yellow label with no title written on it.

A shadow fell over him. "You like VHS?" an older man's gruff voice asked.

Mason looked up at a man taller than he, despite how the other's frame had settled from age. "Yeah, I like the format better. DVDs don't have the same quality."

"Too clear, I take it? Yah, something about that picture quality, it's too sharp. And fuggetabout HD or BluRay."

"Even better if it's a home brew tape," Mason said. "The sound, too, it's like that tishy sound on vinyl LPs."

The man looked at him sidelong. "You one of those hipster kids?"

"Not really. I just like old media. What's the deal with this box?"

"Came from some college theatrical troupe. I do clean-outs on old houses, basements, attics. Found this in the back of the living room in an older woman's house, when she was moving into an assisted living facility. Seems the tapes belonged to her niece, was a hippy-beatnik type."

"So the niece was an actress?"

"Yah, told me she kept them after something happened to the niece. Didn't say what. Told me she wanted it to go to someone who'd appreciate them."

"Think I can give them a good home."

"How's twenty bucks for the box sound?"

"Takes me two hours slinging groceries at Market Basket to earn that. How's fifteen sound?"

"Fair price. Thought you'd beat me down to ten."

Mason took out his wallet, counting out three fives into the guy's hand before the guy handed over the box.

Mason met up with Aunt Melanie near the main entrance, where she had the armoire on a flatbed cart, pushing it toward the open doors and the yard beyond where her pickup truck waited.

"Hey, found some treasures?" she asked. "VHS tapes again?"

"Kid, you like some old stuff," said an older guy watching this.

"Yeah, I'll shelve them next to my cuneiform tablets and parchment scrolls," Mason said.

"Got some good movies?" Aunt Mel asked.

"Some kind of home recordings from a hippy theater group," Mason said.

"Didn't think you were into that sort of thing."

"It's fun to watch and snark at the more pretentious stuff," Mason said. "Shake your head over Shakespeare in a laundromat or something like that."

* * * *

"The heck you got here?" Lexus asked, a few days later when she came to Mason's apartment for pizza and to catch a movie. "God, my grandmother has these."

"Never got rid of the VHS player when DVDs came out," Mason said, hunting up some paper plates.

"So what are these, little kid recital tapes?"

"Some kind of beatnik theater group. Thought we could watch it and have a laugh."

"Really cultured laughing." She pulled up the blank yellow label tape. "This one doesn't have a name."

"Mystery theater. Could be interesting." She handed over the tape. He slid the tape out of its slipcase; the label, also yellow, on the center of the cassette casing read "The King in the Tattered Cloak—Castaigne"

"Sounds like a faery tale."

"Or some kinda Midsummer Night's Dream thing. How 'bout it?"

"Nothing else, we get a nice bedtime story." He slotted the tape into the machine. The drive clacked and pushed the tape out. "Heh. These things can be stubborn." He pushed the tape back in, firmly, the drive door shutting behind it. The player clicked and clacked as the tape heads engaged and the motors started humming. Mason scooted back to plunk down on the couch, cracking open a soda. Lexus helped herself to a slice of pizza and settled next to him.

The screen lit up, a back-lit off-black square, tracking bars shifting at the top and bottom edges. A single vertical line of static danced down the left hand side. The screen jumped to the image of a hand-drawn and shakily printed program cover bearing the title on the tape label now in neat calligraphy, as vaguely medieval music played. The page slid aside, revealing another card, listing characters and cast members playing them.

"Hah, like those 1940s movies," Mason said. "Like someone's turning the pages in a book."

"I always like those, like you're reading a book and playing the story as a movie in your head."

"It's like they went for that look in purpose. If I didn't want to sound all Film-Student-Who's-Watched-Citizen-Kane-Twenty-Times, I'd think it was taped off a TV broadcast."

The play started out as most of these amateur productions did. The costumes looked cobbled together from thrift store finds and bits of fabric in purple and red. The play seemed Shakespearean in scope, if not in language, though it still sounded high-falutin' and literary. It seemed to take place in some made-up kingdom, which they'd given a timeless if vaguely Victorian look, where an aging queen intended to hand over her crown to one of her three children: a kid too young to rule, an elder son too hot-headed to make a half-decent ruler, while the only vaguely competent one, her daughter and eldest child, acted like a dim bulb socialite. Add to this a subplot hinting at some weird cult or the god thereof seducing the elder son.

They'd started on the second act, a scene with a weird old-timey costume party complete with masks (clearly party store domino masks that the costume creators had decked out with whatever feathers and beads and sequins they had on hand). At midnight, the guests would remove their masks. On the moment where the Queen and her daughter confronted an uninvited guest who'd slipped into the party, the screen froze. The tape squealed and the screen went blue. The drive growled and spat the tape out.

"That's odd," Lexus said.

"The hell just happened?" Mason said. "Never had it do that before. Had them shut off and need to be ejected. Had them jam up solid and get stuck, but never making all those noises." He pushed the tape back in, but the drive refused to take it.

"Better than having it get stuck."

He took the tape out and shook it gently before sliding it back in. As before, it would not go in, not far enough to engage the drive heads. "Guess we don't find out tonight which royal kid gets the crown or what the hell Carcosa is."

"What are you going to do with that tape?"

"I know a guy who can fix it. Got me onto VHS in the first place."

Lexus giggled. "Got you onto it. You make it sound like a drug."

"Best legal fix ever."

* * * *

"Probably dust clogging the mechanism," said Davan, studying the yellow label tape.

"Yeah, but it shuts down and the player spits the tape out. Never had a player do that over dust."

"Could be the tape is twisted inside the case." Davan reached for a screwdriver on his work bench and removed the screws holding the back plate of the tape before removing it. "Hmm…"

"Is that a good 'hmm' or a bad 'hmm'?"

"It's an in between hmm. Tape's not twisted. Probably dust, like I said."

"Like *I* said, the jam wasn't like a dust jam."

"Hand me the canned air, it'll probably clear this up in a jiffy." Mason handed over the spray can sitting on a shelf. Davan shuffled the reels gently to loosen them before spraying them, then put the tape back together before slotting it into the player in a rack of equipment near the work bench. The motors hummed and clicked, but the player stayed still.

"It mocks us," Mason said.

"Like it's tensed up. What did you say this movie was called?"

"The King in the Tattered Cloak. Some kind of Shakespeare on meth thing put on by a hippy theater company."

Davan took a step back from the equipment rack. "You serious?"

"Yeah. What's the look for?"

"I thought that was just a made-up story going around on the Internet."

"What, something to scare the kids and the old people?"

"Yeah, it's a creepypasta."

"Something involving scary macaroni?"

"No, idiot, it's a story that gets shared around, copy-pasting style, like a campfire story. In this one, you watch the play, you read the play, hell, you act in the play and perform the whole thing before an audience, you go all kinds of cray."

"And you end up dead after seven days."

"No, you go bug-eating crazy for the rest of your life, saying some tatty king or something else is coming for you."

"Right, campfire story like the guy with the hook for a hand who scratches up your car or hooks you dead if he catches you on lovers' lane."

"Which had it's own grounding in reality. Ever watch that documentary *Killer Legends*? Turns out there really was a guy out killing couples in cars, back in the 1940s or something."

"Weird. But back to the tape."

"If it's locking up, and if this tape is what I think it is, you could be getting lucky and something's protecting your pasty butt."

"Protecting me from what?"

"Whatever it is about the play that makes people go bat crap cray and cut other people. I ain't tinkering with this tape one more minute. I say you dodged a bullet and you leave it be. I don't want you going bonkers and literally chewing Lexus's face. Or your own. I don't want that on my conscience."

"You sound like those crazies that think violent video games make people turn into crazy killers."

"I'm only telling you what I heard."

"If I get any crazy ideas, I'll check into the hospital. Try backing the tape up."

"All right, but here's the part where the genre-savvy friend tells the over-confident protag, 'don't say I didn't warn you'. Do I want to know what you're looking for?"

"Just want to see if the tape loosened up."

Davan threw him a Look, put on a pair of noise-canceling headphones not plugged into anything, then slid the tape back into the machine, rewound it and averted his eyes from the screen as he hit 'play'.

Mason watched the screen, now showing the masked ball scene, the queen confronting the uninvited guest. Behind him, a figure loomed up, which Mason didn't recall seeing during his first viewing.

"Oh crap," Mason said.

Davan hit the pause button. "What? Do I dare look at the screen?"

"I think I saw something in the background that wasn't there before."

"Too much information."

"Maybe I just missed it the first time."

"Maybe it's whatever makes people go crazy when they've watched the thing."

"Or it could be something in the background that looked like a figure."

Davan stopped the tape and ejected it, holding it at arm's length. "If you said it wasn't there before, it probably wasn't there before. I'd nope out of this movie, if I were you."

Mason took the tape. "Good thing I'm not you."

* * * *

That night, Mason had a shift at the grocery store, rounding up stray shopping carriages under the circles of yellow light cast by the sodium lamps in the parking lot. "You all right out there?" Martin, the front end manager, asked. "You've been out there a while."

"Busy day, lots of stray carts," Mason said. "Don't send the search party for me just yet."

Once home after his shift, Mason called Lexus to ask her if she wanted to come over and watch the rest of the play. She said no, as she had a paper due and needed to finish revising it.

"All right, I'll tell you how it ends," he said, shutting off his phone.

This time, he watched the tape more closely, keeping an eye out for the mystery figure, that strange face (if it was a face). No sign of it just yet, no more problems with the tape locking up. The story went on, of the fate of the kingdom on the shore of Lake Hali beneath its twin moons, the devotees of Hastur descending upon the last of House Aldonces. The story ended in a Grand Guignol denouement. He caught himself trying to figure out what techniques this bunch of amateurs could have used to pull it off. It convinced him more than the usual stage blood bags and cow tongue tactics these types tended to use.

It left such impression that the drama went on playing in the theater of his dreams, the insides of his eyelids the projector screen to catch the images. The red streaked figures in tattered garments, limping in procession along the dead shore of Lake Hali, the poisoned trees with their gnarled limbs stretched up to the sky, the two moons and the black sky with the even blacker stars mirrored on its surface, the darkness of the water rippling. The marchers cursed their fate, singing songs in strange keys, crying out wordless curses, emitting retching yowls, their bleeding faces and mouths streaming. The weaker marchers stumbled, falling, the stronger marchers trampling them, grinding their bleeding flesh into the dust of the roadbed.

Mason snapped awake, to sunlight glinting off a yellow school bus chugging below his bedroom window. He looked to his clock, the time telling him he was already late for a job interview at a public access cable station in Andover.

He had a feeling the job was toast even before it started, the way the assistant director asked him the questions in the most perfunctory voice. *I'll be stuck working grocery and helping Aunt Mel the rest of my life*, he thought afterwards as he drove home. *Maybe I can get a gig making commercials for them.*

Busy day moving stuff out of the warehouse-barn behind Aunt Melanie's house and onto the shop floor that took up the whole downstairs, and he took a corner hard while helping her with a sideboard, clipping the back of it and swearing.

Aunt Melanie looked at him with concern. "You all right? You're crankier than usual."

"Yeah, had a rough time with the job interview," he said.

"You sure? You look pale. You coming down with something?"

The knotholes on the wood surface of the sideboard caught his attention, like the eye holes in a mask. He flinched visibly, he realized. "Had weird dreams last night, they kept me awake."

"That'll do it to you," she said, something in her voice sounding unconvinced. "You sure you're okay?

"Might be a bit jumpy over this job interview."

"I know someone you could talk to."

"I don't need a headshrinker, so much as I need a job."

"Well, talking to someone outside your usual sphere can help you feel less frayed about trying to get a job."

"As long as they don't mind me paying by sweeping their office floor or something."

* * * *

Evening shift at the grocery store and Mason spent much of the time bagging or sweeping the floor. Something yellow shifted in his peripheral vision, causing him to jump and nearly knock over a woman's shopping basket on wheels with his broom handle.

"Watch where you're going," a woman in a yellow silk raincoat, pushing the shopping basket, snapped, shoving past him and muttering at the incompetence of the youngest generation.

"Get going yourself, you bat," Mason muttered.

That night brought more dreams, in which he pursued the ragged procession between ruined structures like crumbling castles and temples, bare trees lifting leafless branches to the dust-yellow sky above, more yellow dust rising in acrid puffs from under the marchers' feet where their blood had not yet clotted on the dusty road. He raised his eyes from this rabble to the sky above, to the skyline of the castle where House Aldonces had dwelt for generations, his to claim, as Hastur the kindly, Hastur the gracious, had promised, if he would present a fitting offering.

He jerked awake, the amber light on his alarm clock showing he had several hours left till he had to get up, but lay there unable to fall back to sleep

Next morning, he dragged himself through another shift at the antique shop. "I'll help you pay for a session with Doctor Archer, if it helps," Aunt Mel offered. "If you can't sleep, this is all the reason you need."

"All right, all right, stop twisting my arm," Mason muttered.

She gave him the next day off, sending him to Dr. Archer's office. Mason could see why they would be friends: he could remember when the bookcases that lined the walls of the shrink's office had lined the walls in Aunt Mel's shop, holding up a bunch of Hummels she had trouble moving, along with some encyclopedias in cream colored bindings that had yellowed with age. Now they held up various thick manuals and binders, and a few framed photographs of forests and seasides, likely taken in Maine.

"It's a tough field to get into, I'm told," Dr. Archer, a small man, dark eyes behind silver-rimmed glasses, said. "I'm told there's a high demand for camera crew and film editors, but they're selective in who they hire."

"Too picky for their own good, if you ask me," Mason said.

Dr. Archer cocked his head, the light from the window glinting on his lenses. "You're feeling slightly on edge because it's taking so long to get a job in the field you chose."

"Who wouldn't feel this way? I take it this is the part where I break down bawling because I'll be bagging groceries and lugging furniture up staircases for my aunt, just to pay the bills, and where you reassure me that the right job is somewhere, I just have to be patient, yadda yadda yadda. Insert mommy-daddy-society wound talk."

"You really don't want to be here."

"The hell I don't. I should be out there, getting what's mine, my just deserves," Mason snapped, mind ticking back to the play, the elder son's rant in the first act.

"If you need to let it out, I'm here to listen," Dr. Archer said.

"No. I'm stressed, but I can take it."

"Well, what would you care to talk about instead?"

"Nothing. Anything."

"What do you do when you're not working?"

"I watch a lot of movies. I know, cliché for an AV guy."

"Anything in particular?"

He told Archer about the box of VHS tapes, watching them with Lexus. He didn't mention the yellow label tape or the King in the Tattered Cloak. No point mentioning the dreams. He wasn't sure he wanted to go down that rabbit hole, and have this shrink tell him the dreams meant he really wanted to bang his aunt or something sick like that.

"So you critique these movies?"

"Sort of. Point out what's bad production, learn what not to do. Think of things I'd do to improve it."

"Ah, so more than an MST3K session."

"That's some people's idea of movie critiquing, ain't mine. It's fun to watch when you want something goofy and brainless, but it's too snarky for my tastes."

"In that case, aside from some anxiety connected to the job search, I'd say you're doing well."

"So I don't have to come back?"

"If you feel the need, by all means, but otherwise, go forth and prosper, young man.

* * * *

The light on the answering machine blinked when Mason got home. He played back the message.

"Thank you for your application. We're still reviewing it with all due consideration...." Yaddah, yaddah, yaddah, usual HR blather.

Off to work at the grocery that night, despite the set back. The usual crowd came through: stay at home moms or second shift moms coming in with their ankle biters in tow. Including one not yet old enough for school using the carriage as climbing bars.

"Ma'am, can you not let your child clamber on the carriage?" the words slipping out of Mason's mouth before he could stop them.

"He's not bothering you. Kids need to climb and exercise," Mommie said.

"Yeah, but they're in my way as I repack your carriage." Mason reached over and around the kid hanging from the side of the carriage. He swore the kid moved right into his path to get into his path on purpose. Grabbing a bag with several boxes in it, Mason slung it into the carriage, clipping the kid's shoulder. The kid jumped off the carriage, running to his mother for comfort.

"We got in each other's way," Mason said.

"You did that on purpose," Mommie said, pulling her pup close.

"Wasn't trying to," Mason said, proving her point.

Mommie paid the bill, but rather than going on her way, she approached Petersen the assistant front end manager, talked to him in a low voice.

At Mason's break, Petersen took him aside. "What happened with that kid and a bag of cereal boxes?" he asked.

"What about what kid and a bag of cereal boxes?"

"A woman says you hit her son with a bag of cereal boxes," Petersen said, looking him in the eye. "Was it an accident?"

"Of course it was an accident. You take me for the kind of man who beats kids?"

"You've been a bit more grouchy than you usually are."

"I just got the run around from a job I applied to. It'd put anyone on edge."

"If your attitude here was anything like your attitude at your interview, I can see why they might be reluctant to hire you," Petersen said.

"Whatever. I need coffee," Mason said.

First customer after his break, an old woman who reeked of perfume she'd drenched herself in to cover her stale, unwashed stench. Mason reached up to pinch his nose shut while bagging her groceries—packages of cupcakes and cans of cat food—with the other.

"Don't make the bag so heavy," she said, her S's squeaking through her dentures, as he put a single jar of mayonnaise into one plastic sack and set it aside to open the next bag.

"There's only one thing in these bags," Mason said.

"Don't contradict me, young man."

"Ma'am, with all respect due to your dotage, there is only one thing in each of these bags or two to three very light things. If you see more than one jar in that bag, you need your eyes checked."

"Don't talk to me like that! How dare you speak so disrespectful to a poor old widder woman," the hag snapped, as she raised her cane to brandish it at Mason.

How dare she speak to me like that, he thought and grabbed the cane, yanking it from her gnarled fingers and swiping at her with it. The hag screamed one of those overwrought old beldame screams and staggered backward into the commoner behind her.

He swiped the cane at her head. She shuffled out of the way. "Come back to me, you harridan!" Mason cried, one part of his mind puzzling at his vocabulary before his rage throttled this brief voice of concern. He lunged across the end of the register at her. She shuffled backward, falling into a shopping carriage behind her. The customer hauled the cart backward as Mason reached for her.

"What's going on?"—"The bagging kid's gone crazy"—"Someone find a manager!"—The rest of the line and the customers in the aisle behind them scuttled backward before some turned to run. Mason swiped at the nearest person with his cudgel. How dare they address a member of House Aldonces in such a manner. Let these peasants cower and snivel, he would give them reason to mewl as they did.

A heavy hand fell upon his shoulder. He looked over, his mind briefly registering Famolare, the store director, till he fell back to himself, awakening to the mask falling away, to gaze upon this minion of the dread King, Hastur the Unspeakable, Hastur come to wrench the crown from the heirs of Camilla.

He swung the cudgel to drive off the vile minion, but it wrenched the weapon from his hands. Emitting a war cry, he lunged at the minion. It seized him and dragged him down into the darkness as his head cracked on the yellow floor tiles…

Tuama
by L.F. Falconer

"Did you know I am possessed by an irrational fear of drowning?"

Dr. Chase-Whateley's question catches me off guard. It's the third time in our short acquaintance she's hit me with some random, out-of-the-blue comment. Shivering against the cold sea mist, I glance over at her. "Seems a rather odd phobia for a marine biologist."

"It hasn't always been so Diana, however, it's why I abandoned the sea in favor of zoology."

The captain of the boat grumbles, "It's not the sea ye should fear." He throttles back the engines, the sky overhead the same gunmetal gray as the sea which surrounds us. "And you've still time to change your minds."

Her gaze intent upon our destination, Dr. Chase-Whateley secures the top button of her reefer jacket. "I'm well aware of the legends. I've only come to study the nesting nightjars. The dead cannot harm me."

"It's not the dead ye should fear," the old man mutters.

I'm not certain if Dr. Chase-Whateley didn't hear him or if she simply refuses to honor him with a response. Many are the unfriendly stories rising from this land of giants and ancient gods, one of those being—Tuama only welcomes the dead. I gaze back out at the bleak island we approach, a frigid dread creeping beneath my skin. What did I get myself into?

An area profuse with prehistoric menhirs, stone circles, and barrows, the Kintyre Peninsula remains lost in the Dark Ages. From the farmers to the distillers, its few inhabitants cling to the land like weary ghosts. Off the peninsula's west shore lies Tuama—our destination—a charnel isle which, for five millennia, has sheltered countless bones. Two miles long and one mile wide, the isle is little more than a spit of windswept rock and sand, held in place by the sturdy machair grass. Dead center, its pinnacle rises forty feet above the sea, crowned with the fallen remnants of a druidic temple.

The engines drop to near silence. The boat crawls through the uneasy waters and into a sheltered cove surrounded on two sides by a stern garrison of basalt bluffs. Here, nothing but the past remains. The wrecked. The decayed. The mighty, fallen to the earth, but for one stone monolith which still stands guard atop the headland, forever watching the restless North Atlantic.

The locals refuse to set foot upon Tuama. Dr. Chase-Whateley had to pay the captain of this fishing vessel a handsome sum to convince him to drop us off and promise to retrieve us again when her study is complete. She's curious as to why this isle, and this isle alone, is where the local nightjars choose to nest. Perhaps this anomaly lends credence to the "corpse bird" sobriquet they carry—the keepers of souls.

To spend the month of May living on a graveyard off the coast of Scotland with a woman forty years my senior runs contrary to my idea of a good time. But an internship as a field research assistant to such an eminent scientist as Dr. Miriam Chase-Whateley could hardly be refused. Especially when sugared with a fat check.

The boat skims up to a rickety dock inside the cove. The captain uses his boom to lower an aluminum dinghy filled with supplies onto the beach while the doctor and I unload the rest of our supplies down the gangplank. Never once does the old man leave the sanctuary of his boat. "This is your last chance," he offers before departure.

"I'm only too thrilled to have my feet back on dry land," Dr. Chase-Whateley tells him before addressing me. "Come now Diana, we must secure our camp before nightfall."

I wave the captain goodbye, hoping he remembers to return.

Laden with supplies, we head up the beach toward a large swath of sand near the base of the cliffs. Under the scrutiny of a handful of curious nightjars, their large, dark eyes trained upon us, we work fervently throughout the day. Thwarted occasionally by stiff gusts of icy wind, we complete our campsite just as daylight fails, the sun setting without fanfare. The wind descends with the sun, ushering in a welcome calm.

We lack a generator, and cell phone service is nonexistent. Fresh food will soon become a rarity so I relish our evening sandwiches within the rear portion of the 13' by 27' canvas wall-tent which will house us for the next month.

After our supper, Dr. Chase-Whateley pours a generous shot of Campbeltown whisky into each of our mugs. "Tonight, Diana, we relax. Our real work begins tomorrow." She downs her drink in one swift swallow. "And please, from now on you must refer to me as Miriam. There's no need for formalities out here."

Wishing it were wine, I warm my taste buds with a sip of whisky. Under the bright light of the propane lantern, our shadows loom like a pair of gray giants on the tent wall.

Miriam pours herself another drink. "Naturally, we must study the birds enough to justify the grant."

She's caught me off guard again and I search her eyes for hints of jest. "I assumed the nightjars are why we're here."

"Nightjars…nightjars…I couldn't care less about nightjars." She sips from her mug. "They were simply an excuse to get me here. We'll write down a few observations to satisfy my sponsors, but there's a mystery here much more fascinating than birds."

As if summoned, the nightjars near our camp begin a rhythmic churr, nearly in unison, the cumulative sound pulsating through the air like blood in a vein.

With an animation that's been absent until now, Miriam leans forward. "Tell me, Diana, what do you know of the fourth dimension?"

"I know there are conflicting theories. Many question its very existence."

She leans back in her camp chair, swirling the contents of her mug. "That's only due to the limitations of the ordinary human mind. Yet, in order to attain true understanding from a sphere of cosmic enlightenment, the fourth dimension must be accessible." A twinkle sparkles her eye. "What if I could prove its existence here? Would you like to be a party to that?"

"I'm barely an entomologist. It's not really my field of study."

"Nor mine. And the North Atlantic Avian Foundation would never have given me a dime to seek the fourth dimension. But—to study the birds…" She winks and finishes off what remains in her mug.

While my scientific interests are grounded more in tangible realms, she's piqued my curiosity. "May I ask why you believe the answer is here?"

She stares over toward our shadows on the tent wall. "Few people are aware that when I first met him in my freshman year at Miskatonic U, my husband was a professor of physics."

Who would've thought the old girl had it in her? I lean in, preparing to endure details of her sordid past. "A clandestine faculty/student affair?"

"Oh, no." She waves her hand as if to brush the notion aside. "Nothing so romantic as that. We simply met there. It wasn't until we met again, twelve years later at a symposium in Miami that we got involved. By then I had already made a name for myself in the scientific community, so when we married, among other things, I inherited that dreadfully cumbersome hyphenation of both our last names. But—I digress…"

She leans her aging, lissome form forward, pouring another shot into her mug. "When he abandoned physics and left Massachusetts, Andrew severed all ties with his relatives as well. Yet, several years after we married, he received a gift from a distant cousin, a small locked box not unlike a miniature pirate's chest. For years, it sat unopened and ignored upon a shelf in Andrew's study. I suppose curiosity got the best of him because eventually he broke the lock and opened it." She sighs deeply. "That's the day I lost him."

"I'm so sorry."

She takes a sip and goes on. "He was still very much alive at that point, but he became a man obsessed. The box contained a jumble of maps, journals, and news clippings. He constantly poured over the contents, translating and formulating the information contained within. Near the end, he took to spending weeks at a time within the confines of his study. One day, I went in to check on him and found him dead on the floor near the fireplace. He died of an aneurysm while in the process of burning the box and all its contents. Though it was partially destroyed, the only thing to survive was his own notebook. When I began going through his notes, I grew to understand his fascination. And now," she takes the final swallow from her mug, "here I am, at the gateway of an Elder—"

Something strikes the outer wall of our tent. We both leap to our feet, looking at one another in mutual confusion. The wall is thumped again. And again. Then once more.

Snatching up a flashlight, Miriam darts though the partition into the front portion of the tent. I scramble to follow. I don't want to be left alone. The thumps against the tent continue. Miriam rifles through an equipment crate, finally coming up with a small pistol which she'd somehow managed to smuggle through. She shoves an ammo cartridge into it, instructing me to grab the flashlight. My hand shakes as I pick it up and reluctantly follow her outside, deriving a shallow sense of security from the Swiss army knife in my jacket pocket.

The pulsating songs of the nightjars vibrate the very air, giving the area a false sense of life, as if the island itself is a beast ensconced in deep slumber. Warily, we round the tent's front corner. The beam of my flashlight washes the wall.

Lowering her gun, Miriam laughs. "It's only the birds. They're feeding."

In the darkness, our tent walls glow from within. The air is thick with insects. Swarms of beetles and moths cling to the tent walls while nightjars wheel about and bounce off the canvas, plucking the choice morsels off.

Like a pair of schoolgirls, we share our relief with laughter and make use of the latrine while we're out before settling back into our tent. Miriam snuffs out the propane lantern, immersing us in utter darkness.

"We'd be well off to keep our activity confined to daylight hours or we'll be overrun nightly with unwanted guests. Sleep well, Diana."

I settle into my cot. Within minutes, the thumps against the tent walls wane. Eventually, the churring outside tapers off, leaving little more than a whisper of waves lapping the nearby shore. As I drift off in the ensuing silence, from deep within the sand beneath us, I swear I hear a distant moan.

* * * *

After breakfast, Miriam tasks me not only with collecting and identifying insect specimens, but with the mounting of an infrared camera inside the populous nesting grounds as well.

"Be careful where you step," she warns before wandering off with a charred notebook and a GPS device in hand, her pistol holstered upon her belt. Last night's levity has vanished. This morning she's all business.

As if forced to make an unwanted appearance, the sun looks sullen today. It's difficult to maneuver around the nests, and whenever I snap an insect into a jar it stirs up a flurry as the birds attempt to draw me away. The eggs resemble small pale pebbles upon the soil, nearly invisible to the untrained eye. When undisturbed, the birds resemble stones as well—thousands of rounded dull brown stones nestled among the surrounding grass and black basalt boulders. Stones with large, obsidian eyes, ceaselessly staring.

I suspect I'm only here to provide Miriam an appearance of propriety, gathering data on insects and birds while she's off searching for the fourth dimension. If she should succeed, will she truly include me in her discovery? Why would she if I'm not by her side? I have doubts it even exists, but what a legacy that would be! Yet here I am, scrubbing for bugs which could easily be plucked from a tent wall in the night.

The collection of more insects can wait. I close the specimen case to scope out a suitable location to mount the camera. As my movement ceases, the birds hush, their assiduous surveillance over me unnerving. Other than the wave action on the shore, the sudden silence wraps me up so tight I'm afraid to breathe, to make any movement or noise. *Afraid to be heard?* There's a fraction of taint in the air, an odor of decay and rot, the undeniable stench of an ancient tomb. Despite the protection of my jacket, the brumal breeze turns my blood to ice.

I glance back at the lone stone monolith which overlooks the sea like some grieving widow whose husband failed to return from his voyage. I wonder for what, or for whom it's waiting. I'd like to investigate it up close, but it won't be today. I need to catch up with Miriam before she disappears from my sight completely.

On an island bereft of trees, I have little choice but to mount a post atop one of the hundreds of barrows that give the island its name. They dot the land in small grassy mounds, from round to oval, giving the illusion of a rolling, hilly landscape. Similar barrows on the mainland have dated back as far as 3000 B.C. It seems profane to drive a stake into a burial mound yet atop a mound will give us the best vantage point for filming.

Threading my way through the minefield of nesting nightjars, stirring them back into action, I locate a suitable observation spot. "My apologies," I whisper, bringing my hammer down upon the mounting post, driving it into the earth. As if I'd driven the stake into a living being, at this very moment the island shudders, nearly knocking me off my feet. A rumbling groan gurgles up from deep within the soil.

The unexpected seismic activity leaves me breathless. It's a hasty job accomplished with shaking hands and a racing heart, but I manage to get the infrared camera mounted, aimed, and the timer set. Snatching up the tool bag and specimen case, I hasten toward the center of the isle to catch up with Miriam.

The nightjars only nest on the lower grounds, leaving the hillside free and easy to navigate, the only impediment being the abundance of grass-covered barrows. Zig-zagging around them, I'm slightly winded by the time I approach Miriam near the hillcrest.

"I've noted a distinct lack of predation here," I tell her between breaths. "The ample food and lack of natural predators are likely the main factors—"

"The gateway is up here," she interrupts, cutting me to silence. "I should have known it would lie within the temple." She shoves her GPS device into her jacket pocket but keeps her notebook in hand, heading further up the hill.

"I guess it makes sense that the druids would build a temple on such—"

"You give them too much credit," she admonishes. "The druids may have made use of this temple, but they certainly had no hand in its construction."

Shaken by another small tremor as we approach the crest, Miriam doesn't miss a beat.

"When humankind was barely out of infancy," she continues, "too young to comprehend what they were incapable of understanding, their superstitious minds deemed this a place of magic when, in fact, it's simply part of natural reality. Mankind simply needed to mature in order to understand and make proper use of it."

Devoid of grass, the crest is littered with toppled pillars of ancient Lewisian gneiss. I wonder how they were brought here, who actually brought them, and why they no longer stand. At one time surely they'd stood as proudly as those at Stonehenge, yet now lie in disgrace, though not necessarily due to time or seismic tremors. They appear to have been felled purposely toward the center of the circle, completely blocking any access.

"It's a shame it collapsed," I dare to voice my opinion.

"What's truly a shame, Diana, is that Andrew attempted to deny this to humanity. But great knowledge does not come without its price, and he paid his."

She steps to the end of the nearest stone slab, a full six feet tall, equal that in width, and probably fifteen feet in length.

"Be a dear, Diana. Climb up top and give us a look."

I've never been adept at rock-climbing but set my tool bag and specimen case aside. After locating several suitable hand and footholds, I lug my way up to the top face while Miriam whispers what sounds like a prayer. The stone seems to shift as I stand and I shake off a momentary lightheadedness. The distinct stench of Tuama is thick up here, yet awestruck, I suck back my breath, then slowly release it, holding strong doubts these stones ever stood upright.

"Miriam, you really should see this." The stones are laid out perfectly, like the spokes of a wheel, wider at this outer end, tapering slightly as they converge around the empty, center hub. This is too precise to have been accidental. But why have I never seen pictures?

The little girl inside of me who used to hide under the covers during lightning storms fully resurfaces, urging me now to run away. Run fast. Run far. Fighting against retreat, I glance back. Miriam struggles to work her way up but I won't help her. Since she was adamant that I come up here ahead of her, I fully intend to get the first look.

I force my feet toward the center and peer down, immediately inundated with a potent, vertiginous rush, and swiftly kneel to keep from tumbling over the edge. Below, where the bare earth should be, lies a deep chasm of cosmic darkness swirling with phosphorescent gaseous whorls in druzy black velvet, as if viewed straight through the lens of the Hubble Telescope. I'm gazing into another existence—one beyond all words, beyond time, and into the well of infinite knowledge. A gateway to the fourth dimension. What was a moment ago nothing but unproven theory has become unmistakable fact.

Though dizzying, it draws me in for a closer look. Behind me, Miriam's voice drifts through in some uttered litany with guttural words foreign to my ears. The cadence raises an ominous dread in my soul. Before I can respond, the air crackles, electric. All sound disappears beneath the rise of ten thousand nightjars shooting into the sky to blot out the sun, ushering in a false twilight. The discordant din is deafening, their shrill and harrowing cries competing with the booming roar of air rushing beneath their wings.

Disgorging violently from underground comes a resonant groan. Beneath me, the massive stone heaves and shifts. I cling to the rock to keep from plunging into the cosmic well. From the depths, a nauseating gas spews up, a stench so foul I can only envision a fetid cesspit into which a thousand decomposing bodies have been left to rot.

I lived the majority of my life in San Bernadino on the San Andreas fault. Whatever this is, it's like no earthquake I've ever experienced before. It feels so much more "alive."

A tarry ooze rolls up from the depths at the heart of the wheel, flooding our surrounds with a fathomless, stygian sea, undulating jellylike beneath the splayed stone slabs. Earth vanishes, the sky overhead blackened by birds, the stones inconceivably buoyed above the influx of dark waves. In the focal core, bubbling to the surface emerges a bronzy, serpentine thing, fully ten feet long, followed by a dark orb, faceted with plate-sized hexagonal cells resembling monstrous ommatidia of an arthropod's eye.

I scuttle back with nowhere to go, surrounded by the putrescent black liquid that sloshes and slurps hungrily against the sides of the stones. The monstrous eye rises, peering over the edge of the stone, the bronze antenna sinuously waving in the darkened air.

"I'm sorry, Diana." Miriam's voice echoes as if she's miles away.

"By the love of all that's holy, what is this?" I gasp, whirling around. Catching sight of Miriam, I melt into the stone. Her face ashen, she kneels beside her journal at the far end of our impossible raft, her pistol drawn and aimed directly at me.

"Great discoveries come with a great price." She keeps the gun steady with both hands. "I had to bring you, you see. It's nothing personal. But according to Andrew's journal, the gatekeeper will need to feed."

It takes several moments for her intent to hit home and all I can do is glare in gaping disbelief. But, the cold-hearted bitch is going to have to shoot me because there's no way I'll go willingly into this horror show.

At this moment, our impossible raft keels sharply to the left and I cling for my life. Rising like a breaching whale, a segmented, plated crustacean shell, gleaming metallically, arcs up through the ebony liquid—a leviathan bronze deviant nearly prehistoric in nature. It rolls to the right, further rocking our float, exposing countless centipede-like legs.

Dozens of jointed limbs latch onto the stone, glistening like patent leather on the aboral side, the ventral sides laden with rubbery tubular protuberances which walk across the stone with smooth, hydraulic movements. Every leg joint sports two barbed, writhing tendrils that crack the air like whips.

We've no place to go, trapped like deer on an ice floe.

One of the tendrils snaps out, coiling around my ankle. Beneath my jeans, my skin burns like a brand.

I scream. The nightjars scream. From the far end of the stone, comes another scream. Miriam's.

Another tendril lashes out, wrapping around my left wrist.

Recoiling, I yank back. It squeezes tighter. Eight gunshots ring out. Instinctively, I duck, and the tendrils pull me toward the edge of the stone.

To no avail, my fingernails claw at the leathery flesh wrapped like a tourniquet about my wrist, my hand burning and swelling as the flow of blood is cut off.

Wriggling my free hand into my jacket pocket, I locate my pocketknife and slice the inner corner of my mouth while prying it open with my teeth. The taste of my own blood fuels my fury as I slash at the tendril above my wrist.

All at once, the nightjars hush. There's no time to ponder why, but without their clamor, all that remains are slurps, slithers, and Miriam's frantic mewls and howls.

Repeatedly, I slash at the tendrils that bind me, alternately between the one at my wrist and the one at my ankle. A black wave swells, heaving the stone into a precarious slant. I slip closer to the edge.

Slashing desperately, again and again and again, I'm nicking much of my own skin in the process. The ropy tendril above the coil about my wrist begins to bleed, exuding a milky green mucous as noxious as the fetor at the center of the wheel.

Gagging back my retch, I continue to hack at the tendrils until I cut through enough to wrench my wrist free. Several more slashes and the tendril above my foot tears apart. I squirm back, away from the edge.

"Help me!" Miriam cries, sliding toward the far edge of the stone, firmly entangled within a grisly clutch of tendrils. Her right hand still grips her gun, the left one outstretched, her eyes pleading with words she cannot utter.

I scoot across the expanse and reach for her. Our fingers touch. Interlock. Then, with a deliberate, unconscionable calm, I let go and draw my hand back. "It's nothing personal," I say. *The gatekeeper needs to feed.*

The tendrils drag her off the stone, plopping into the inky jelly below. Miriam froths within the black sea, her eyes wide and white with terror until her screams drown inside gulps and inaudible burbles.

She disappears into the murk and the turbulence grows still. Only a scathing silence remains.

Encased within raw cold, I cannot move.

Dear god, what have I done?

The nightjars screech, piercing the dead silence. The ebony sea drains into the earth leaving the ground dry and unblemished, the monstrosity within vanquished. The nightjars break away, releasing the recalcitrant sun. The stone which buoyed me rests haphazardly upon the barren earth, the precise layout of the stones no longer existent. Only the burning remnant of a tendril still coiled about my wrist assures me the experience was not hallucination.

I struggle to peel the remains from my flesh. It clings as if it had teeth and leaves behind bloody gashes as I finally wrest the leechlike tendril from my skin. Flinging the gruesome thing as far away as I can, I watch aghast as it wiggles and burrows like a worm into the soil.

Easing myself down off the stone, I warily test the earth with my foot. Do I dare trust its solidity? Nearly hidden in the stone's shadow, Miriam's notebook lies abandoned in the dirt, the only evidence of what truly happened here. I inch my way to it and snatch it up before forcing my feet to take me back to the shore, grateful they still obey.

They come to an unbidden standstill when I near the base of the hill.

Here stands a fresh mound of soil liberally laced with the earthy stench of Tuama. It had not existed when I passed this way on my ascent. No grass grows upon it. The meager sunlight gleams off the barrel of a pistol poking out from the dank dirt of the island's most recent barrow.

Tightening my grip upon Miriam's journal, I note the last few pages had been completely consumed by fire. What horrible truths had been burned from existence?

Dr. Andrew Whateley was right to attempt to destroy it. I only wish he had succeeded, for humankind will never be mature enough for the eldritch knowledge it contains. I bury the book deep beneath the fresh soil. Tuama can keep her secrets.

The nightjars watch. They stare with accusatory knowing. Unblinking. Unmoving.

I will be glad to be free of this isle of tombs. But what will I say about Miriam?

Reaching the dinghy, I push the small boat into the water, scramble aboard and begin to row. The Kintyre Peninsula mainland is little more than a mile distant. I can see it, beckoning like a mother to her lost child.

I can't stop shivering and there is no warmth in the sulky sun. My oars smack desperate and hard against the water. Overhead, the sky darkens. Like flies drawn to the dead, nightjars swarm around the dinghy. A flash of bronze skims the crest of a turbulent wave. The boat tilts. Above, spotlighted within a beam of sunlight, a lone stone monolith stares out at the sea—a sea turning black as the night, reeking with the undeniable stench of an ancient tomb.

Mercy Holds No Measure

A Tale of the Bajazid

by Kenneth Bykerk

There is an old oak tree that stands sentinel before a drum of curious design on the backside of the mountains men today call the Bradshaws. Hidden behind a thick copse of manzanita, there stands a convex disc four feet in diameter and formed of a rough skin, a pliant bark taut and wrinkled with glyphs almost perceptible, in the wall of a small canyon, an insignificant gully at the end of an unnamed wash. At the center of this drum, an eye within concentric rings of discordant display, lies an artifact of a most unusual nature. At first glance one might imagine a pearl or a piece of ivory stained and yellowed, a chip of well-worn antler or a kernel of quartz stuck in the center of that shield. It protrudes but barely and quivers ever so slightly with an uncertain rhythm, a beat too low, too soft to register the air with sound.

* * * *

He had had enough. Of all the professions he had tried in his years, this he determined was perhaps the loneliest. He didn't mind the solitude, at least to a degree. He had always worked in the company of others but the further west he had come, the more he became accustomed to such quietude. When that time alone stretched beyond normal bounds, when the company of others was denied for a week, a fortnight or more, then he began to chafe. He began to regret his self-imposed exile and determined he had had enough. Some men are hermits by nature and some just in passing. For Samuel Delrosa, the allure of hermitage had long since passed and it was time to return to the world, any part of the world as long as it was far away from this damned hole in the ground.

He had tried to lie to himself that it was the nature of the work which led to this decision but the lie wouldn't take. There was much more to it, including that which he had hitherto refused to give credence but now was uncertain about. True, it was back-breaking work in at times the literal meaning. He had been fortunate so far and he knew it, especially considering his lack of knowledge of what he was doing. He had never shied away from hard work and lack of knowledge, he reasoned, could always be improved upon. If talent or inclination didn't take hold, he could always reassure himself that the endeavor in question was never really for him in the first place. This had led to an odd assortment of jobs over the years, none of which had taken root. Hard-rock gold mining? He knew now that he was not meant to be a miner, just as he knew he was not meant to be a farmer, a carpenter, a butcher, a rancher or a dozen other things he had tried on his way west.

When he was young, before he ever needed to shave, he swept the floors and cleaned and carried and stocked at a local market in his neighborhood. He could have built a steady income for himself as he was much favored by the owner but he was restless and saw the life of a shop-keeper dull and routine. When he was old enough for the hiring manager at the docks to notice him, when he had the stature at last of a man, he quit the store and started in as a lumper. Two seasons on the docks and he was convinced that was not the life for him so he headed to a foundry and learned, very quickly, that the life of a caster was even more undesirable. To the stockyards he went and after six months as a knacker, he was ready for anything else but the ceaseless gore of a slaughterhouse. As if in answer to his prayers, a fort in far-off South Carolina was bombarded and a call was put forth for able-bodied men. He quit the stockyards and signed up for a new slaughterhouse and a new career he very soon wished he hadn't pursued.

He spent the whole of the war doing things he never would have thought of doing and never would have wanted to. He went in wide-eyed and adventurous but was cured of that quickly. The life of a soldier, even that of an officer, was not for him so he learned to avoid promotion. He wanted out but if he had to be in, he did what was needed, pulled his weight, and lost count of friends fallen. Eventually he found himself in a long march, a victorious rout to the sea and through attrition and longevity, ended the war with stripes on his sleeves. He was lucky, extremely so and he knew it. He had faced and returned fire more times than he cared and survived scarred by neither battle or disease. He also learned how to fight.

When one puts on wander-legs in their youth, going home to jobs already determined detestable is the least of options. There was a world out there that was now accessible so he stepped out to discover what his life's work would be. He had a little plunder he had picked up on the way, an investment program he instituted on the road to Atlanta. It was enough to give it a go on some good land in Kansas vacated in the recent troubles and with no heirs to resist or complain.

It was a very educational year. He learned he knew nothing about farming. Where his neighbors' crops came in full and ripe, his modest field yielded exactly two dozen viable ears of corn. He knew he was the laughing-stock and talk of the community, unwelcome by nearly all sympathies as an outsider and considered unlucky to even speak to. Even those who had worn the same coat in the recent conflict wondered openly, him at times mere feet away, if the previous owner of that land was not getting his due at last. Such speculation ended in Delrosa taking a deep depreciation, but one he was willing to in order to never till a field again. He purchased a kit and a brace of Colts, mounted up and never looked back. He had learned, beyond all doubt, that he wasn't meant to farm the land.

Wichita was a busy place, one with ample opportunity, especially for a man in his prime who could hold his own. Boom towns always need men to build the next saloon or the next bank. Dozens of odd jobs as well were to be had for one unafraid to work. That kept him busy with a roof over his head for nearly a year but he was young yet in a town that did not have sidewalks to roll up. It was during this time he learned that he was no good at cards and that hard liquor was not something he handled with decorum. More than once he was rolled, either drunk in an alley or in a prostitute's crib. When the roof over his head began to worry his pockets, he determined it was time to move on.

From Wichita ran many trails. It was the Chisolm he took, signing on for a life in the saddle. No more roof to shield him from the weather at night. This did not bother him in the least for he had years in the field of just that behind him. This was hard work of a new nature, one with left him often riding on the fringes of the herd alone. That was when he first felt the stirrings of loneliness. In all his previous occupations, he never worked alone nor was ever truly alone. Whether the docks of Lake Michigan or the construction boom in Wichita, he always had worked with others in teams or pairs or at least with others within view. Even as a soldier, with exceptions of nights on sentry, he had always been surrounded by others. On his farm, he worked alone but he was not far from others and a regular procession of the morbidly curious had turned the road alongside his sad little farm into a well-traveled trail. Out on the range, he found himself riding solitary for long stretches of time. While there had been jobs he had detested, with the exception of farming, there had never been one he couldn't do. The work was good and the moments of solitude were welcome and reflective. The worst part of life in the saddle, he determined, was the saddle. Some men are born to them. He had not been.

At Fort Worth, the drive was over and after a week hard in whorehouses and saloons, he was ready to ride again. There was word of a drive heading west from Fort Belknap. With some of the men he'd ridden the Chisolm with, he headed west, a Yellowboy '66 over his saddle. It was well before the Pecos he learned that he'd made a mistake. This was a hell run across the deserts of west Texas and up New Mexico ending in Denver.

Not only was the Goodnight-Loving near twice as long at least as that of the Chisolm, it was through wastelands haunted by Comanche and baked by the sun. They were ambushed more than once in what amounted to mostly harmless harassment raids. Delrosa knew how to fight and did but he was learning that this wasn't the life for him; work related injuries due to Comanche arrows was not appealing and life in the saddle left quite a bit to be desired. He rode and he fought and he endured and the very moment the drive was over, he collected his final pay and said good-riddance to an ever-aching ass and life on the trail.

Denver was a raw and rough town yet. Hiring on as a carpenter was no problem, at least short term. He figured with the long list of trades he was building, at least he wouldn't starve before he found his proper calling, something that he could imagine his life doing. Construction wasn't where the money was though. Silver was King in Denver and the mines were paying so he said goodbye to the sun and crawled underground for the first time. Hard work but different only in the manner. He worked hard, sweated hard and learned what he could, adding it to all the knowledge over the years he had obtained. Along with that he added mining to the list of things he preferred to not spend his life doing. There had to be a better way and after a winter spent digging in the heart of a mountain for another's profit, he left Denver and the mines to further seek that better way.

He rode as a hired gun with a wagon train heading south and west. The Arizona Territory was the destination. He didn't know or care what or where Arizona was. It was a place and he was displaced. Loneliness began to take over even when the solitude was welcome. All whom he had known in his life were no more. The city of his youth was no longer home and the men whom he marched with were either dead or in the wind. He rode distant and aloof, preferring his own company to that of the settlers he was being paid to guard. Even the other bulls on the train he avoided where he could. When they reached Fort McDowell and cashed out, he took stock of where he was and what he had. The middle of nowhere with very little was the answer.

He was in a desert he would never have believed the likes of which could have existed had he been described it a decade before. In nearby Phoenix, he found work helping to dig out ditches they said were ancient Indian canals in a mad scheme to water the desert. It took him all of three weeks of sun-blasted heat and scorpions crawling in his boots before he mounted up and rode north, and it was only May. The talk around the trading posts and saloons had all been of gold. Everyone, it seemed, knew someone who had struck it rich or so they claimed. Tales of floats lying in the open, gold nuggets the size of a thumb there for the taking if you just found the right hill or the right stream. There was talk of a Dutchman and his mine in the Superstitions to the east. To the north, one creek in particular was the chief focus of gossip; the Bajazid in the Silver Mountains. The tales coming down from there were near unbelievable. It was discovered, the stories went, with gold lying glistening in the sun, the stream fairly sparkling. That party that found it were all rich as sultans. A rush was underway as those Sultans, a title assumed, could not stem the flood of hopefuls looking to find their own fortunes. That is how he found himself in Baird's Holler.

He arrived in Baird's Holler in early June of 1871. It was a respite from the desert floor below, but barely. Pine forests covered the mountain canyon but did little to mitigate the heat. The town as well was hot. Four years from the founding and the town claimed seven saloons but only two houses of worship, and neither of those were complete in construction. His distrust of others was amplified in this place. Of all the places he had lived, all the sites he had seen, Baird's Holler is the one civil setting which most reminded him of the chaos of battle he had known. Fights in saloons and in the streets by tired, desperate, drunk men were daily occurrences. He saw two men gunned down his third night in town and a body swung on the lone gibbet the fifth morning. That night he got into his first brawl and walked away with only a bloodied nose from a fist that landed before he pummeled the other guy into unconsciousness. He did not hold his decorum well with hard liquor but that did not deter his drinking. He was surrounded by men lost and alone like himself and each and every one eying the other with warranted suspicion.

He stayed in a common room for two weeks before his Winchester was stolen. After this he sold his horse and saddle to save livery expenses and took a single room in a boarding house. It cost, but the privacy, the solitude and the safety was worth it. He had taken a position on the courthouse construction and had a little money to spare. This evaporated nearly as quickly as it came in. He was alone in a boom-town, surrounded by hundreds of men just like himself and each hostile to the other. He drank with those he worked with and at times joined in their brawls. He took to bed many a woman but only after paying. By the end of the summer, he had had enough and began to take exploratory hikes through the surrounding canyons just to get away from other people, just to be on his own. He felt trapped in town and could feel the general hostility around wearing thin on him.

That October, when at last the heat was beginning to abate, he took one of his hikes. The Bajazid runs east to west in general direction. Five tributaries feed it, three from the north and two from the south. It was along the lower southern creek, a gully off a side canyon, where he found the nugget. He had been out a day and had already slept one night beneath the stars. Aggressions he hadn't known had been surfacing and he figured a couple days on his own would perhaps prevent him from killing someone. The nugget was lying amid loose rock out in the open, something that at least confirmed tales he'd come to believe were too tall to bear. Searching around, he found more small chips and nuggets and traced their general source to the back of the gully. He had no idea what he was doing beyond blindly digging, but he started in with the small hammer he carried on these outings just in case. An hour later, he sat staring at a small handful of gold in the palm of his hand.

He purchased some proper picks and shovels. He bought a shotgun and shells. He picked up some provisions. He overpaid for a mule to pack his possessions and, taking leave of his room and his employment, established a camp beneath an oak tree at the back of that gully. Prospecting was new to him and his experience in mining was from the standpoint of a cog in a large machine. Here it was just him and he began chasing into the side of that gully hints of a vein revealing itself just enough to inspire pursuit. He sought nuggets, chips, flakes; that which he didn't have to process but could just pack away. He knew he was abandoning valuable ore as he dug. His inexperience he recognized and he figured, if he needed to, he could erect a simple arrastra and grind the ore down. He set aside large chunks to do just that but the vein he was following was providing enough solid pieces that he kept digging and let the ore pile.

After two weeks, he went to town with a couple baskets of ore which he had assayed to sell. While this proved some for his pocket, his true treasure he kept hidden back at his mine. He spent two nights in town taking advantage of a bed to let, a choice of saloons and a whore of his picking. On the second night, he never made it to the whorehouse. While pissing in an alley, a short, rat-faced man came up and distracted him enough he didn't see the giant come up behind him. He woke that morning aching but he woke in the bed he'd let. He'd left the big fellow unconscious and laid out in the mud. The rat-faced man he had to kick multiple times in the stomach before he stopped struggling. He had taken a beating himself as well but not anywhere as bad as the two who had jumped him. He knew how to fight.

Back at his camp the next day he discovered his claim had been found out when he was gone. His tent, a simple canvas sheet strung between the oak and a nearby pole pine, had been uprooted from two of its grounding stakes. Nothing, to his surprise, was missing but someone had been there and had violated his property. It wasn't a beast for the footprints in the dirt were clear. Whomever had struck had a lame, dragging gait.

He did not return to town for another fortnight and that became his pattern. For meat, rabbits and squirrels taken with his shotgun sufficed. Other than that, he had hardtack and beans enough. Footprints would sporadically appear near his camp, whether coming as he slept or when he was deep within his hole. They were consistent, a dragging step where one shouldn't be. He began to sleep with his shotgun beside him, an ear always listening for a step that he never heard. This left him on edge, paranoid constantly and assuming he was being watched with intent to rob. When he did return to town it was again to have ore assayed. Of the nuggets he had been prising from the ground, those he kept in a saddlebag which he taken to hiding within his tailings. He had no desire to carry his prize with him and risk it to thieves such as the pair he'd left in the piss and mud of that alley. He saw those two again on that trip to town and on others and they recognized him as well. Whenever he saw them, the rat-faced man and his lackey, he made sure to expose the handle of his Colt Navy. Five miles is a long trip when the contours of the land double the distance traveled. He stayed the night and returned the next morning with supplies to his camp unmolested beyond that same set of mysterious tracks again in the dirt.

He killed a man the next time he went to town. He was followed on his return by two unartful enough to track properly. At first he thought it was rat-face and his large friend so he hid and waited for his assailants. It wasn't who he expected but the result was the same…he was being stalked by a pair looking to exploit him. They hadn't planned a parlay and he gave them no chance to make such a case. Startled, they drew when he announced himself. Gunfights last seconds. He was left with one dead man and a trail of blood from the fleeing second. He did know how to fight. He abandoned the corpse where it lay and finished his return to his mine never knowing what happened to the other.

For five full months, he dug deeper and deeper. Each day he dug, the worse his disposition grew. Of all the places he had lived, never before had he been so distanced from his fellow man. Never before had he felt such disdain, distrust and outright hatred for others. When he visited Baird's Holler, which he did roughly every other week for supplies, he would notice only the ugly, only the coarse. The town was growing and an extremely mild winter allowed for continuous construction. The town had boomed, a quarter at least larger than it had been then when he had staked his claim, but he didn't notice. He saw only the rough edges where men shed their skins and clawed through their drunken desires, the shadows where beasts prey on each other after the drudgery of the day is done. For five full months, he dug himself deeper and deeper into his hermitage and abandoned the world save to refill his reserve and his bottle.

Once when he arrived back at his claim following a trip to town that March, he saw that it had been plundered. All that was missing was a good quantity of the ore which had stacked up. His personal effects had been ransacked but being he had nothing much of value exposed in his camp, his loss was minimal. His growing stash was where he had hidden it, inconspicuously buried under stones beneath a small patch of manzanita which grew between the oak and the entrance to his mine. Inside the mine, the bandit had done him a favor of removing some large pieces of ore for him. To his dismay though, the bastard had also taken his shotgun which he'd hidden deep within. He was tired of this place.

He had had enough.

This realization came to him as he crouched uncomfortable at the back of the tunnel he had dug. It wasn't an impressive tunnel. It reached a depth of only about ten yards and averaged four feet in diameter, enough to facilitate his entry and work. Throughout it was supported by braces of wood, either made from young pines chopped himself or lumber purchased in town. The result was a tunnel only the ignorant or truly brave would find comfort in.

For the last time that morning his head made intimate contact with a sharp rock lodged in the earth above him. His back ached from the posture he was forced to assume and his knees, exposed through threadbare slacks, showed the abuse of months upon them. This was enough. This was not the life for him. There had to be a better life out there, something better than the slow destruction of his body and soul scratching out an existence that was not worth living. He was sure of this and over the months, the memory of his earliest employ merged with observations made on his road west to inspire his last resolve in this hell-hole he had dug.

Since he stepped onto the docks at 17, he had worked hard and strenuous jobs when not spending time staring down rows of blazing guns. He had always gravitated to the most physical or demanding professions. He realized that the men who had the money weren't the ones doing the hard, physical work. He didn't mind such work, not at all, but he wasn't wanting to do that forever. In every town he'd passed through on his way to Baird's Holler, and even there, the one person he always had to at some point visit was the local general store. The proprietors of such were always the same, regardless personal appearances. They lived with roofs over their head. With this in mind, he worked the earth those few months, worked it and steadily prised a significant fortune from that vein. He kept his treasure in that saddlebag which was nearly full, and this he kept banked in the side of the gully beneath a few significant boulders dislodged from his tunneling and cleverly hid behind that scrub of manzanita. He had enough, surely, to begin such a life for himself somewhere. Open a dry goods market perhaps…but not here, not in Baird's Holler.

He had been daydreaming of a mythical place further west where a peaceful ocean sent cool breezes over a warm, sun-kissed paradise. A dry goods purveyor with a comfortable routine could live a pleasantly dull life in such a place. He had his start-up, both in his saddlebag and the leather pouch he wore around his neck in which he placed the nuggets he would cull as he dug. He had enough and had planned just one more quick scurry in the hole before packing up his mule and heading out. He would avoid Baird's Holler completely, his distaste for it complete, but head north to Prescott. There he'd figure out how to get to California. Just a quick look down the drift to grab a few final nuggets or chips or flakes. Every little bit would help. Then he hit his head just one too many times.

He began to back out of the tunnel. At that depth, he had no choice. It was his freshest push and he hadn't widened it to fit yet. As he edged backwards, a glint caught his eye. He leaned forward with his feeble wick lamp and sure enough, there was a sizable nugget lying right in the open he'd missed. How he'd missed it, he couldn't imagine. It was larger than any he'd picked in the last week and he'd just scoured that area with hand and eye before calling it quits.

With muted oath, he reached forth for the nugget. When he tugged at it, it yielded. It was heavier, larger than it appeared with the bulk buried. This got his interest and he nudged his way as close as he could with the flame held forth. About the nugget, which at this point showed the size of Minie ball, was a small pool of glistening surface, black like oil. Where it came from he knew not for it was not there one headache ago. He pulled at the nugget and it began to ease forth ever so slightly. It was jagged allowing him to hook his finger around part to gain purchase. The more he pulled, the larger it grew before his eyes. Twice the size, now thrice and all with a steady pull. He grabbed the nugget firmly, the tips of his left-hand dipping into the inky fluid, and pulled.

Out it came, twice yet the size last visible, black goop stringing between the chunk of gold and the small puddle the nugget came from. He flicked his wrist and pulled, freeing the nugget from the oily slime but sending one strand swinging back and looping around his hand. He casually wiped his hand on his pants as he squinted in the dim light at the gold before him. Nodding in satisfaction, an unexpected bonus at the end of his last hour in the mine, he opened the pouch and stuffed the nugget in. Yes, he was done.

He stuffed the pouch back in his shirt where it lay over his heart. This brought his left hand close to his face. The scent of the oil on his hand was delicious. It hinted of berry, but one unfamiliar to his tastes. He sniffed his hand and then stuck out his tongue to timidly taste this syrup he'd stumbled upon. It was as delicious as it smelled so he tasted a pool of it gathered on his wrist. He looked back at the little pool and froze. There was movement in the pool or around it, he could not tell. He drew his lamp closer and there, on the surface of the pool, rose dozens of thin stalks, pitch as the pool itself and indistinct from it. Some rose as high as three inches before they would bubble at the top, swelling to burst in miniature explosions of mist. Then the stalks would collapse and reform, the fallen cannibalized to form the next to fall. Then one stalk kept rising. It failed to bubble but twisted and writhed, a perverse, blind tendril seeking his hand.

He scrambled backwards in abject terror. In panic, he twisted and turned there at the narrow end, where his body had no room to turn and twist. Through sheer panic he contorted his body around, his feet dislodging one of the simple braces he'd set. As he scrambled, the earth collapsed down upon his trailing leg, crushing it between freed stones. He screamed, and as he did so, the sweet berry on his tongue turned to putrid flesh. His stomach revolted and he choked on his bile while trying at the same to draw breath to scream. He was left coughing over a pile of vomit, his right leg trapped beneath unstable rock.

The collapse had been isolated, only sealing off the very end of the tunnel. The black tendril, that thing that reached for him, was on the other side of the cave-in. He had traveled enough by sheer terror to ensure this separation, or so he hoped. His foot was trapped though. He could feel where his shin was pinched, where it was trapped between sharp stones. He could move and wiggle his foot a little, the limit being the available space. He also took heart that he did have some control over his foot. He could wiggle it. Now if he could just figure out how to get out of there without bringing more down on him, or at least ease his leg enough to pull his foot through. That was his intent but he was having trouble still heaving emptily over the vile pool beneath him. He could not get the taste of rotting flesh and unclean earth from his mouth.

Then he felt a scratch, a purposeful movement against the heel of his trapped boot. It was the slightest of pressures, the faintest touch, but it was not where or how such should or could exist. Behind him was nothing his sane mind could conceive making such a gesture. No animal, no beast or serpent or even insect he knew was behind him under that collapsed portion of the tunnel. All that was behind him was an insanity in writhing ink and his imagination could not grasp what possibilities there might be. He froze, cold sweat on his skin and a taste of fungus and forgotten flesh in his mouth, horror at the impossible unknown building to a pitch as the probing focused on a spot. When the scraping and scratching stopped and the pressure on the heel of his boot intensified at a point, that horror erupted and panic seized him. He pulled, he twisted, he dug with his hands furiously but he could not budge his leg from the trap it was in. All the while he could feel that black thing, that inky, amorphous awl steadily boring through the heel of his boot.

He was soaked in sweat and vomit, his panicked exertions having occurred without concern for the pool his stomach had left. His breathing was labored and his air growing short with wheezes between his gasps. His fight was giving out. Whatever it was that slowly assaulted his foot had delayed its advance enough that he began to ease in his concerns allowing the exhaustion of adrenaline spent to take hold. He looked up to the entrance of his mine and saw the oak tree framed. The sunlight played on the leaves, a light wind orchestrating their dance as they mocked him with their freedom. He pulled and twisted and strained once again for naught as he reached out his hand for that distant oak, that receding freedom. His perspective of the tunnel was shifting, his vision lengthening as the adit shrank and his eyes focused on the ruin of his outstretched hand.

The tips of the fingers on his right hand were corrupted with pustule growths while black fuzz sprouted from the backs of his fingers. He brought his left hand forward to catch what light he could. It was worse, much worse. Where the black tendril had touched, a thick, scaly surface was forming with white pus beginning to show between the plates. As soon as he saw this infestation, it began to itch intensely. He thought of his mouth immediately and realized the taste in his mouth wasn't a mere memory lingering. He had been too focused on the fear slowly working the heel of his boot that he'd taken himself for merely parched. It wasn't thirst and the aftertaste of vomit but worse and as he realized this, he heaved again and again and again though only a few small chunks of blackened bile fell forth. And of that pool of vomit, further horrors he saw for it stewed and swirled of its own, bubbles forming on its surface only to pop in fine mists. Wherever that bile had been splattered in his frustrations, stalks were growing in every ichorous color or puffballs deathly white began to bloom. He was infested from within and covered under his own bile. The unbearable itching seized dominance. He tore at his flesh without mercy with hands themselves enraged. A new frenzy took hold, his exhaustion unable to contain the panic and this new level of discomfort.

There was no respite. There was no collection of moments wherein he could pause and reflect. Mercy holds no such measure in the maw of mindless malevolence. The drilling on the bottom of his boot ceased with the surrender of the sole. With that he froze again, the discomforts of his deterioration swept aside as expectation dreaded the absence of that steady drill. Horror anticipated is worse than horror known in the experience of the lucky or the secure. Anticipation is but a phantom though when horror reaches beyond the bounds of sanity and backs up its promise with shrill and direct pain…and pain it was.

He felt a point like the tip of a needle press against and then pierce the thick callous on the bottom of his foot. Above all else, he felt that needle slide into the flesh of his heel. He felt it reach in despite his frantic exertions, his kicking and thrashing, and bore slowly through the sparse meat to the bone. His screams were choked, his throat raw and rotting. Chunks of flesh and fungal slime flew from his mouth as his eyes shed all pretense of sanity. He thrashed violently as the needle forced its way through the bone of his heel. It bore, this dread spike, and he raged in helpless pain until he crashed his head into a rock above and plunged into a restless oblivion.

When he woke, it was to the sweet taste of exotic berries and the hope that he'd had but a dream. He lay there with his eyes shut savoring the warm comfort which enveloped him and the soft pillow beneath. He had memories of pain unbearable and horror beyond bounds but now he lay on a soft pillow of…rotten meat. He opened his eyes in dismay as the soreness in his leg and foot returned in a dull, throbbing ache. He was unmoved in his tunnel and the angle of shadow on the oak beyond the adit told of a setting sun. Beneath and around, his mattress had grown, a fungal padding blanketing the tunnel. The nausea returned but he had no stomach to purge. When he did heave, he choked on the growths which had taken root within. He choked and gagged and spat until a hint of air reached his tortured lungs. He struggled at his leg but was too weak to accomplish even a pretense of effort so he lay his head down and cried.

Samuel Delrosa knew he was doomed. Even were his foot not trapped, even were he to crawl out of that hole right then, he knew his damnation was assured. Something inside him had turned. That horrid black pool had poisoned him, that he knew. It had infected him and it was rotting him from within and without as he watched. He could see the boils rising and popping on his arm, spreading infection at a visible pace. The corruption didn't hurt beyond a low and enduring itch across and within the whole of his body, an itch that would demand attention were it not the least discomfort present, were it not his least lament. He lay there weeping for his loss, for his life. He wept for the future promised by the saddlebag he had hidden and the pouch tied around his neck, that engorged bag of gold pressed beneath his heart. There would be no cool breezes off pacific waves. There would be no future, no comfort of friends found or families formed. He knew he was doomed and wept for the loneliness which he knew was his. He wept until he almost found peace in the rhythm of his suffering.

It was as if a child inexpertly plucked at the strings of an untuned harp, the string being the nerves that ran through his wounded leg. First the flesh around the hole in his heel began to burn as if acid had been injected with the needle. Then the bone that had been bored cracked as the tendril which had pierced it pulsed and bulged and grew. And then, as he his eyes shot wide and he choked on the loosened lining of his throat, that finger of black plucked at his sciatic nerve. It plucked once again, then slid as if a roughened bow over strings up his leg in staggered movements. It did this for a perceived eternity, a direct and intentional assault on raw receptors until once again the host lay unconscious and oblivious. His contractions and exertions through the ordeal left him with weakened bones in arms and legs cracked under the sheer pressure put upon them by muscles contorted. The pillow beneath his head now included more than just the contents of his stomach but much of the stomach itself.

When he woke, it was to the scent of sweet berries and a warm sensation in his crotch. He almost hoped. He never had the chance. Death filled his nose and choked his mouth. Anger inflamed every nerve within his groin. He tried to scream and more came from his mouth than he could clear. When, after hours of this singular torture he still hadn't drawn breath, his dismay and fear became complete. His tormentor was cruel. This thing which gripped him, which had bored through his foot and twined itself around his every nerve, knew no such thing as mercy. It was cruelty manifest, eternal anger and malevolence unbound. It had no name, none he could understand but he knew it now, knew the reason he dreaded this valley. Knew that until the end of time here would reside this perdition, and until the end of time he knew that his tormentor would tease him such.

In this eternal solitude, the loneliness of an undying soul, he suffered. He felt his flesh blister away to feed that rot which he had become. He watched the days turn to weeks as the sun played upon the oak outside, the tunnel filling more and more with the odious growths until at last his sight was lost and his eyes, unneeded, dissolved to his unabated agony. Every second of every existence he gasped and sucked for air but he knew he had no lungs with which to breath. There was a beat, a throb which resounded from his chest, but it was only the pulsing, burning nerves twined tight around a heart of gold. All that remained of Samuel Delrosa were his nerves stretched throughout the tunnel in mockery of their former frame, inflamed and cruelly caressed by tendrils of black ink and malice. And his bones, his relics, they spread slowly throughout that mass, pushed by the noxious growths which sprang from his flesh, pushed to their destined reaches; the light at the end of the tunnel. There, at the head of the fungal flow, there only did he succeed in reaching that open, free air. There only did the tip of one finger, trembling to agonies unending, poke through that horrid drum trapped behind a bramble of manzanita which grew wild around an ancient oak tree at the back of an unnamed wash in mountains of central Arizona.

Treacherous Memory
by Glynn Owen Barrass

Her new client had chosen a conspicuous spot for a meet. Intentionally so, if Cassey had interpreted his manner on the telephone correctly. Ted Cruise had sounded paranoid and scared.

The place she waited outside was called: 'FIKA Espresso Bar,' a quaint looking café built below a brownstone. The café was painted black, the name written in large silver metal letters above the front window. The area fronting it was dedicated to outside seating: red metal chairs and tables lined the sidewalk, protected from the vehicle traffic by a barrier of small bushes in large rectangular iron planters.

The seats were filled with people talking to one another or into cellphones. It being the end of summer, with an autumn chill already in the air, many patrons had their coats and jackets on.

Cassey could feel the encroaching cold through her own jacket, and held her paper cup of espresso two-handed, relishing the warmth. She was halfway through it now, and Ted Cruise was late.

Cruise where are you? He had called the night before with a tale of a missing wife who had disappeared two years earlier. She had reappeared three weeks ago, claiming a complete lack of memory for the missing time. He was concerned about her. Selene was acting differently, and in ways that frightened him.

"Two whole years," Cassey said, staring at the diminishing brown foam inside her cup. Her theory was that Selene had left him for another man (or woman), and with that new life having failed somehow, had returned to him with a story of amnesia. *People don't just disappear to nowhere; she'll have left traces, definitely. And is that what Cruise wants me to find?*

"Er hi…Are you Miss Bane?" A shadow crossed the table.

Cassey looked up. The voice she recognized, but the owner was of course, new to her.

He was tall and thin, dressed in black slacks and a thick grey woollen coat. His complexion was pale, which enhanced the dark stubble on his face. His dark brown hair was mussed up, like he had just gotten out of bed.

"I'm Cassey Bane yes," she said, and waved at the empty seat facing her. The man was getting stares from the other patrons, and just before he sat, he glanced around suspiciously.

"Mr. Cruise, I take it?" she asked.

He nodded, his lips forming a hint of a smile.

"Want a coffee?"

He shook his head. "Not right now, I'd just rather get down to things." Cruise looked behind him, scanning the other patrons again. He turned back to Cassey, reached into his coat's left hand pocket, and removed a black iphone. Placing it on the table, he went to tap the screen, hesitated, and placed his hands in his lap.

He's pretty spooked; I'll give him that.

"I told you the history of things on the phone," he began, "Selene, the Selene that came back, it's not the same person." Another look around, then he reached for the iphone, touched it to illuminate the screen. "She hasn't been back long, and there's just something…Better I show you." He turned the iphone around and pushed it a little way towards her.

Cassey leant forward, curious, but had a little trouble working out what she was seeing.

"That's Selene's left shoulder blade," he explained. "Look closer. You see the scars?"

She looked closer, and yes, the pale skin bore an array of small white dots.

"I took these while she slept," Cruise continued, "They're on both shoulder blades, the calves too…" A tap on the screen showed the back of a left leg, what looked like a yellow bed sheet beneath it. There were more dots on the calf. He drew the phone back across the table.

"There are others, in, err, more intimate places, but I didn't have a chance to photograph those."

"That's…that's alright," Cassey said, a little embarrassed at these can-did shots of his naked wife. She took a swig of coffee, swallowed and cleared her throat.

"Have you asked her about them?"

Cruise shook his head. "She says she doesn't remember, and pushing her doesn't help. Also, there's…" he lowered his voice and leant forward. "I've woken up to find her undergoing these strange spasms at night. And as for the memory loss, her memory is even cloudy about events from be-fore she disappeared."

That is interesting, unless she's faking it, just like the loss of two years.

"Where exactly did she disappear from, Mr. Cruise?"

"Call me Ted. It was after we'd been camping in the Vermont Woods. The night after we returned, she disappeared from her bed. The police were involved of course, but nothing came of it until she reappeared on our doorstep."

"Ahuh." Apart from the mystery of the scars, and the fits, this was looking more and more like her original hypothesis was correct.

"Alright then, Ted." Cassey drained the rest of her coffee. "I have all the information I need for now, so in my capacity as a private investigator, what would you like me to do?"

Cruise stared at the table for a moment then looked up. "I'm away from the house most days, working at my brother's garage. She does go out though, a neighbour told me."

"So you want me to see where she goes, huh?"

Cruise nodded, "That would be a good start, yeah."

* * * *

Half an hour later, Cassey was back in her office and about to start typing some notes into her laptop. As her fingers touched the keys, her cellphone began to ring. The noise came from her scuffed, tan leather jacket, hung behind her on her chair.

She reached around to the inside pocket, gripped the cellphone, and lifting it out examined the screen. The word 'ABE' stood out on the screen. Pressing the answer icon, she tapped the speakerphone function before placing the phone in front of her laptop.

"Hey Abe, any luck?" she asked, and began typing up the details of Ted Cruise's case.

"Hi Cassey," the voice replied in a strong Brooklyn accent. "I found his place of work, what I thought was his place of work, but it turns out he was fired over a year ago."

"Huh. He told me he worked at his brother's garage."

"I spent a good hour talking with one of his ex-colleagues, up here in Guttenburg. He worked at an advertising agency, place called Science & Information Inc."

"That's a long way from his new job. You said you were talking with the guy for an hour though? Spill the beans," she said with a smile.

"Well it wasn't all about Cruise," Abe explained, "His ex-colleague is a Rangers fan, and you know how I like talking hockey. Anyway, according to this guy, after the wife disappeared, Cruise became obsessed with alien abductions, lost his job for taking too much time off etcetera."

"Oh," Cassey replied, and stopped typing.

"You alright Cassey?" Abe said after a few moments of silence.

"Yes and no," she explained. "Cruise seemed odd when I met him, nervous, jittery, but he never said anything about aliens. Damn. He could well be a nut."

"Pistachio or Wall?"

Cassey laughed. "No, the batshit crazy type. Anything else Abe?"

"That's about it really. The guy said he felt sorry for Cruise, but was glad when I said she'd returned."

More than I can say for Cruise himself, Cassey thought, then said. "Okay Abe, and thanks. Email me your expenses and I'll transfer the money over to you."

"That's great Cassey. Always a pleasure. Do you need anything else doing on this case?"

She thought about that for a moment, then said, "That's it for now."

"Okay Cassey, have a good one."

The connection was severed, and Cassey remained still for a short while, absorbing the silence around her while she put her thoughts in order. She returned to her notes, revising them as she read what she had already typed.

Background to the case: Ted Cruise, aged 38, contacted me on the 25th of August with the information that his wife, who disappeared 2 years previously, had returned to him three weeks ago. Selene Cruise, aged 32, who disappeared after a camping trip to Vermont, apparently has no memory of where she was during that time.

I met with him today (the 26th). He suspects his wife has changed in some way, and disclosed photographic images of dot-like scars on her shoulder blades and calves. She also has trouble remembering events from before her disappearance. He informed me he works in a garage through the day, and that his wife goes somewhere unknown while he is out.

From new information I have obtained, from a former work colleague at the company Science & Information Inc, it appears Cruise is interested in alien abductions.

Cassey paused, rested her fingers on the keys. *I guess he thinks aliens took her*, she thought, then started a new paragraph.

Possible leads: Find information on who dealt with the case originally (Vermont State Police?), and get their opinion on what happened to Selene. I will arrange a second meeting with Cruise and enquire about her social life and friends from before she disappeared.

Hypothesis: I suspect that when Selene 'disappeared,' she started a new life, and has now returned to Cruise using faked amnesia as an excuse.

She stopped typing, scanned what she had written, and satisfied with it, directed the laptop's curser to the 'Save' icon before closing the document.

I might solve this quickly by following her, she thought, *and it won't be connected to aliens either.*

The rest of her day was taken up with other cases. The biggest involved putting the invoice together for a surveillance job she had been on for over a week—spying on an employee his boss suspected was stealing from him. That wasn't the case, but she still expected to be paid, all the same.

Tying up the loose ends on two cases she wouldn't be paid for took up the remainder of her time. One was a surveillance job, spying on a wayward daughter. The client, the woman's mother, had died during that case. Cassey had found the woman's corpse, and didn't have the heart to pass charges on to the next of kin. The final case was a favour for a dead man.

Professor Arthur Peabody, a man she consulted with on numerous occasions before his death, had left a letter asking her to destroy some artefacts he had in storage. That 'favour' had nearly led to the loss of her and Abe's lives, plus a week in the shop for her car.

Before leaving for the day, she phoned Cruise and asked if he would be at home tomorrow. The answer being no, Cassey resolved to get started on the case the next morning.

* * * *

The Cruises had a house in Maplewood, New Jersey, a thirty-six minute drive from her office that including travelling over bridges spanning Upper and Newark Bay and an interstate drive to Maplewood. The Maplewood area appeared quite picturesque, with large gardens fronting its two-storied detached houses.

Her silver Toyota Venza was parked directly across the street from number six, the Cruise house partially obscured by trees lining the sidewalk.

Past the sidewalk, and a raised path flanked by a garden of lush greens, the first floor, clad in cream stucco, held a white door between two white-framed windows. The second floor had three windows beneath a grey slate roof.

Cassey had been waiting for twenty minutes now, with no movement evident from inside. She had a flask of coffee with her, her digital camera, and the resolution to get the case at least partly solved today.

Ted Cruise owned the only car in the household, so wherever Selene was going, she either walked or got picked up.

Twenty minutes later Cassey was still waiting. Fifteen minutes after that, she checked the time on the dashboard against her cellphone. Both were synchronised correctly to twenty-five past ten. Cruise had left for work at nine-thirty, just before she arrived. According to him, Selene usually left the house soon after he departed, or at least, so the unanswered house phone indicated.

Selene could have left in the short time between Ted's departure and her arrival. She hoped not, for that would mean a long day of waiting. Or, today could even be an exception to Selene leaving at all.

"Well, in for a penny," Cassey said, and reached for the flask on the front passenger seat.

At eleven oh two, she saw a woman walking down the sidewalk across from her, heading in the direction of the Cruise house.

She had long, reddish-blonde hair, grey joggers and a matching hooded top. A black plastic bag dangled from her right hand. The description Cruise had given fit, and when the woman paused before the garden, Cassey told herself it was Selene.

I guess she did slip out after all.

She retrieved her camera from beside the flask, put it to her eye, and began snapping off photos.

Selene walked into the garden, stepping over the plants to disappear momentarily behind a tree. After reappearing, she continued her progress then paused before the left-hand downstairs window. She looked up at the second floor window, then knelt and reached inside her black bag. She removed something from it, tucked whatever it was into the greenery, then began digging in the earth. A few minutes later she appeared done. She stuffed the black bag into her pants pocket and headed towards the door, rubbing muck from her hands as she walked.

A moment later she opened the door, which was unlocked, and disappeared inside.

"Curious," Cassey said, and lowered the camera to her lap. *What is she so intent on hiding? Drugs? Only one way to find that out...*

She opened the car door and stepped stealthily across the street. Moving low, she reached the sidewalk, and slowing down stopped behind a tree. Seeing no movement at the house windows, she continued on, entering the lush green of the garden. She watched the house, the door in particular, as she crept. A few seconds later and she was at the spot where Selene had paused. Going to her knees she felt around, her gaze still set firmly on the front door.

Her hands felt soil, the thin stalks of plants, and then she touched something solid, planted into the earth. She gripped it, and pulled. The object, whatever it was, felt solid in her grip. Any moment now, she was expecting Selene to come rushing out. It didn't happen, and after a few more seconds of stillness, Cassey turned and made her slow way across the garden and the sidewalk. Using a tree to conceal herself, she looked down to examine her prize.

"What the fuck?"

What lay her palm resembled some kind of shell, a bulbous, roughly circular pink object about six inches in diameter. It was covered in light brown nipples, which in turn were surrounded by short, stubby pink spines. Vertical regions of undulating lavender lines divided the nipple areas into four, the lines terminating at a top bearing a smaller, squashed sphere. This bore small stubby spines and lavender zigzags, leading to a brown nipple at its apex.

Cassey stuffed it into her jacket pocket and stepped across the street to her car. After a few vigorous hand rubs to remove the soil, she reached for the handle and climbed inside. She closed the door and removed the object from her pocket, placing it on the dashboard.

What the hell is this thing? It looks like a seashell but... Cassey lifted it up, examined it from different angles to see if there was some way to open it. There was nothing visible, and the bulbous top proved immovable when she tried twisting it off.

"Huh," she said, and placed it back on the dashboard. It was looking more likely that Mrs Cruise had a screw loose. Deciding to wait and see if Selene did anything else untoward, she reached for her flask.

* * * *

Her day of surveillance had been a bust. Selene hadn't made another appearance, and when it got close to four p.m., and the time Ted Cruise was due home, Cassey headed back to her office, leaving the shell in the glove compartment in her car. After calling Cruise and arranging an appointment the following day, she left for her apartment and was home just before six o'clock.

An evening of relaxation was cut short when just after nine, her cellphone rang. She was laid on her couch, dressed in pyjamas, her laptop on her chest as she indulged in some online shopping.

Thinking it might be Abe, she reached over and retrieved her phone from the coffee table beside the couch.

The number on the screen wasn't Abe's but it was familiar. It was Ted Cruise.

"Hello?"

"Please you gotta come here," he said in a loud, hurried tone. "I didn't know who else to call."

What the? "Mr. Cruise? Ted? Calm down and tell me—"

The call cut off. Cassey sat up quickly, moving the laptop from her lap as she did.

An attempt to contact Cruise returned a busy dial tone. She paced the room and tried again, with the same result.

Seeing no other option but to check on him in person, she headed to her bedroom to dress.

Thirty minutes later, after teasing the speed limit at every opportunity, Cassey was back in Maplewood.

She hadn't brought her gun—that was still in her office drawer. As she pulled up outside the Cruise residence, she regretted not making the time to retrieve it.

All the windows of the house were illuminated. Cassey stared at it for a few moments, then unclasping her seatbelt, exited the car, leaving it unlocked behind her. Her cellphone, gripped tightly in her right hand, brought a little comfort as she crossed the street towards the garden path.

The foliage on the left side of the path was heavily damaged. There was even earth and plant matter scattered across the path. *Selene*, Cassey guessed, and looking to the front door, saw that it stood slightly open.

She stepped nearer, paused, and nudged it open with her left hand, allowing it to creak inwards on quietly complaining hinges. Before her lay a blue doormat, dirty with muck, and a cream carpet bearing brown marks that led left. With slow, careful steps, Cassey walked past the threshold into the house. The walls and ceiling were bright white in colour, with varnished oak doors upon the west, east and north walls. Each stood wide open, spilling light and silence. An ascending staircase stood beyond the east wall, white with cream carpet covering the steps.

The house appeared so quiet. *I need to call the police. That's what I'll do.* A sound from upstairs, a strangled cry, stopped her from raising her phone. Instead, she rushed to the staircase, ascended the steps three at a time.

The upstairs décor was similar to the downstairs. To her left, beyond a white wooden handrail, stood a wall centred by an oak door. Framed countryside prints flanked the door. To her right, lined up with the facing wall, a narrow corridor led to darkness.

Another sound, a low moan, returned her attention to the door. She turned left and crept towards it. It stood slightly ajar, with light showing within the gap.

A few moments later Cassey was pushing the door open. Inside she encountered a terrible scene.

Selene was laid out upon a thick, light brown carpet, her arms and legs splayed. Dressed only in her underwear, she had on pink panties, a black bra. Dirt coated her bare feet. Her head was bent sideways, pointing right, her eyes open and glassy.

A double bed with a black iron frame stood to Cassey's right, the yellow sheets and pillows in disarray. To her left, beyond the corpse and between two pale wooden closets, was the window facing the garden.

So where was Cruise?

"Please."

The voice issued from the corner to the bed's right. Cassey turned and saw Cruise crouched there, his back to the room. Dressed in a red polo shirt and black pants, he was barefooted like his dead, murdered wife.

He shook where he crouched, his hands covering his face.

"Ted, what have you done?" Cassey asked, and took a few tentative steps towards him.

He raised his head to reveal bloodshot eyes, a tearstained face.

"Keep away from me," he said, his words tinged with fear.

"Seriously Ted. Tell me what happened."

He looked away, sobbed, then turned his red-eyed gaze back to her.

"She started freaking out about an hour ago, after she'd been in the garden." Cruise shook his head, sniffed loudly. "She attacked me. It was self defence, I swear."

"Arrrrrrrrrrrrrrrrrrrrrrrrrrrrrrrrrrrkkkkkkkrrrr."

The sounds, a strange combination of hums and clicks, came from behind her. Cassey turned quickly, and saw they issued from the woman she had presumed dead.

"What the?"

"Kkk-kk-rrrrrrrrrrrrrrrrrrrrrrrrrrrrrrrrrr," the sounds continued, stuttering in a strange mechanical way.

Movements behind Cassey told her Cruise was rising from the corner.

"She's alright!" he said, and went to squeeze past her.

"Stay back Ted." She held out her hand, halting his progress. The fine hairs on her arms were standing on end.

"Why? She—" Cruise stopped talking. His wife's head turned to face the ceiling.

Cassey felt a weight in her chest. Something unnatural was happening here. She guessed Cruise felt it too for he backed away quickly.

Selene went silent.

The lights flickered. Selene's mouth snapped wide open with a 'click.' The lights flashed again, then went out.

The following scream made Cassey drop her phone and cover her ears in pain. Even then it overwhelmed her, sending her down to her knees.

Selene's voice was more akin to a siren than anything a human being could produce.

The light from outside, meagre as it was, illuminated Selene's shadowy form. Cassey stared at her, her fingers gripping painfully into her scalp. Then, to her added horror, the woman's chest started to pulse.

A dark shape filled the window, and the glass exploded.

Instinct made Cassey duck her head, small pieces of glass hitting her hair and back as she curled herself into a ball.

A deep, bass-filled buzzing sound, even louder than Selene's wail, filled the room.

Cassey heard something clamber in through the broken window, a noisy scraping followed by a 'thud.'

The buzzing was so powerful it made her teeth rattle. She was absolutely terrified. An animal whine escaped her lips.

The drone wavered, then formed words. "Time to end this. The probe is broken."

Thudding footsteps followed, footsteps that paused terribly close to where she crouched.

"Not yet. We can repair it." This, another buzzing voice, came from the doorway behind her.

"What of the others?" it continued. "This interference is unwanted."

More thumping followed, from both sides of the room.

"Neutralize the male," the first voice said. "The other bears observing, after some adjustments."

A heavy, vibrating object touched her head.

"Sleep Cassandra," the unseen horror said, and the noise and fear disappeared.

* * * *

When she considered how insistent Cruise had been for her to help, Cassey felt annoyed at this sudden cancellation. The text had arrived a few minutes after her arrival at the FIKA bar, and read: 'Sorry Ms. Bane. All is resolved now. Bill me the hours.'

She hadn't bothered replying, yet. Rather, she sat drinking her rapidly cooling espresso while thinking over her day so far.

Even without this, her morning had been a bad one. Her car had been broken into overnight—nothing of value taken, just a smashed window and some ransacking. Then there was her laptop, dying as soon as she powered it up in the office.

Most of her files were backed up on the Cloud, so only those pertaining to Cruise were gone, and what loss were they, really?

"Might as well get back to other cases," she said, and retrieving her cellphone from the table, dropped it in her inside pocket. *But there's something I'm forgetting here. What is it?*

Cassey shook her head. She swallowed the rest of her coffee, rose from her seat, and left the café.

The Hutchison Boy
by Darrell Schweitzer

Caleb Hutchison was over at our house, playing video games with my son Jackie the night the world ended.

It was cold that evening. Late October at the New Jersey shore is not exactly beach blanket weather, but there was Caleb at the front door of our cottage as he always was, dressed in rags that must have been adult cast-offs, a checkered flannel shirt that fit him like a tent, with the elbows out, and baggy jeans torn off just below the knees; he was barefoot as always, which wouldn't have been unexpected for a beachfront in July, but in thirty-something weather with the wind howling and spray and maybe even sleet ratting against the windowpanes, and him sopping wet with his pale, wispy hair plastered to his head, and himself so appallingly skinny that his limbs looked like pale, bluish sticks, the result was that before he could say more than a faint "Hello" my wife Margaret had screamed, "Oh my God!" and hauled him off to the bathroom, where after a minute or so I could hear the shower running and steam poured out from under the bathroom door. Then the hair drier was going, and by the time she produced him again Caleb wore a pair of borrowed jogging pants and a sweat shirt that drooped down to his knees and a bathrobe over that and fluffy slippers, and only *then* did he manage to blurt out, "Can I play with Jackie now?"

A minute later you could hear the two of them laughing over the assorted beeps, whistles, and explosions from the game console in the TV room.

The borrowed clothes were actually mine, because, for all he was about the same age as Jackie, twelve or so, Caleb was a full head taller and his build was so different from that of our rather short, chubby offspring that nothing of Jackie's would have fit.

It occurred to me that Caleb hadn't been shivering. Margaret had described him as "cold as ice" but he hadn't seemed the least bit uncomfortable.

"*Where* are that boy's parents? That's what I want to know," Margaret whispered to me angrily.

It was a good question. I didn't have an answer.

"That kid's got some kind of weird skin condition," she added. "I've never seen anything like it."

I just remained silent.

It was later that night that the power went off, and never came back on again. I don't think it ever will.

* * * *

As for the question of where Caleb Hutchison's parents were, the answer was they lived somewhere north of us along this remarkably undeveloped stretch of southern Jersey ocean front, past what the kids called Dead Man's Cove for its alleged piratical associations, a swerve of shore and bend of bay which was actually *rocky* along its edge—unusual in these parts—so that it was more practical, especially at low tide, to wade across than make your way around by land, particularly if you were barefoot, which helped explain why Caleb usually showed up at our place wet; which explained nothing at all, really, such as why Caleb showed up at all, but I confess I was not paying attention.

Caleb had become Jackie's new best friend that summer. I was glad for that, because Jackie was picked on at school and it was good for him to have a friend at all, even a weird one, even if they made a Mutt and Jeff or Laurel and Hardy type pair. (Caleb, oddly, knew those references. Jackie, of course, did not.)

Could I *meet* Caleb's parents sometime, like maybe when I drove him home some night?

No, there wasn't any road to their place. Caleb always left on his own, wading along the water's edge, even if it was very late.

Besides, they were busy with their "church."

We were different, I knew. I and my family were summer people. They were all-year-round people, though I gathered, not native New Jerseans, but originally from somewhere much farther north, some place in New England I'd never heard of, whence the family had fled years and years ago after the Great Persecution of 1927, whatever that was.

(I tried to look it up on Wikipedia. Nothing. Another of Caleb's stories. He was full of stories.)

Okay, so my son's best and only friend and constant companion was this weird urchin whose parents probably belonged to some even weirder cult and probably chanted gibberish while sacrificing nude virgins; girls, I hoped, which would leave Jackie safe, and Caleb too; and this is where I admit that I'm selfish and a bad parent and neglectful—though never abusive toward my own kid—because, you see, our presence at the Shore that year was not entirely a vacation. I was trying to work. Here I was the alleged Highly Artistic Novelist, the hottest thing since Thomas Pynchon, and, for all I lied non-stop to agents and publicists and editors about How Well The Book Was Coming, the truth of the matter was I was tearing my hair out and completely empty of ideas and writing shit that I couldn't show anyone. Margaret was a teacher of languages nobody cared about, who was about to be laid off from the Philadelphia school system, and, oh by the way, an up-and-coming part-time professional photographer who suddenly seemed to be a no-timer because she couldn't get any assignments. So you will appreciate that the two of us were . . . under a considerable amount of stress for our own vain and petty (not to mention financial) reasons, and when we were not on the phone, begging or cajoling or telling outright lies, we were all too often screaming at each other, enough so that she said we needed counseling and I said she needed a shrink or maybe just a lobotomy. And for all, in some deep, inner drawer of my brain I still loved her and Jackie and wanted everything to be happy the way it once was (in our imagination at least), there were surely times when I concluded that my whole life up to this point had been a mistake and I should have remained unmarried and become a shoe salesman.

A sure thing. I mean, everybody needs shoes, right?

Except maybe Caleb.

The deep dark secret, I think, is that Margaret likewise was glad Jackie had a friend, for all the right, maternal reasons, but for all the wrong ones too. Translation: it got him out of the way so we could fight with each other and not have him see it.

May and June, I heard a lot about Caleb at the dinner table, but I hadn't met him. Margaret seemed to be in on the secret well before me; maybe she had; maybe, I sometimes suspected this Caleb was a collective hallucination between the two of them, the kind of imaginary playmate who told Jackie the most remarkable things. I mean, why else would a twelve-year-old who liked video games, comics, and Japanese animation be asking me if there really was a golden city under the ocean near here, a place with shining pillars, where fish-men lived forever and worshipped a god that looked like a giant frog?

No, I had to admit, I didn't know anything about that.

Maybe it was something he got out of the comic books, which, I understand, have become a lot more challenging than they were when I was Jackie's age, or maybe it was the anime, which never made sense to me anyway.

But Caleb knew all about that kind of thing.

And there was that night when neither Margaret nor I had noticed that Jackie was gone until it was almost dawn, and we caught him sneaking back into the house, and he admitted that he'd been out on the beach with Caleb, looking at the stars where they "opened" (which was apparently Caleb's phrase) and making marks in the sand with sticks that somehow glowed (whether the sticks, the marks, or both, I am not sure) while talking to voices from out of the air.

That we didn't do anything, that we just let things proceed without any intervention, I feel guilty about now. Yes, it was bad parenting.

It must have been about the first of July that I came home from what I was pretending was a research trip, and there was supper on the table, and an extra place set because we had been joined by the elusive Caleb, who smelled of seawater and was barefoot and wore cut-offs and a ripped tank-top that fit him so badly he looked damned near naked in the thing. My first thought is that this is the kid who is so skinny that when he comes into the schoolroom sideways the teacher marks him absent, and my second was that I wondered if he ever went to school. The next thing I did was give him an old Philadelphia Phillies t-shirt of mine, which fit him like a night-gown, but he put it on and gravely said, "Thank you, Sir."

Oddly, for a kid who knew how to say "Thank you, Sir," he also gave me the initial impression at dinner that he didn't know what a fork was for, but he was a good mimic, and sly about it, and I could tell he was watching us before he did anything, and after a minute or so he definitely had the hang of it. He ate ravenously too, everything Margaret could feed him, but it was like all the food went into hyperspace, not into his stomach, because it never seemed to make him even an ounce heavier.

But when he started to talk, I forgot all that, even as I forgot I was talk-ing with a twelve-year-old at all. I began to wonder if Jackie's new friend wasn't the next budding Einstein, because he did mention hyperspace, and something about "angles in space-time" and the stars being "right" and a lot of stuff I just couldn't follow at all. I glanced over at Margaret, and she looked blankly back and shook her head, but, incredibly Jackie, who had never been very good at school, seemed to have some idea what Caleb was talking about, like it was a private language between them; and they *did* use some gibberish words between them, a little furtively, which definitely were *not* English, maybe something from that weirdo church that Caleb's parents belonged to.

But then dinner was over and the two of them ran off into the TV room and they were just kids again.

That summer, you will recall, was the Summer of Strangeness, or the Time of Signs, or whatever you want to call it. There were lights in the sky at night, which nobody could explain, sometimes great swirling spi-rals of color that would last until dawn. Sometimes the stars themselves seemed to ripple. The pundits and the papers and the internet were full of talk of UFOs and the Second Coming and gravitational disturbances, solar storms, and whatnot. It was also a time of storms on Earth, and after Super-storm Obed wiped out Miami and New Orleans pretty much for good this time, and the sea level rose even faster than the Global Warming alarmists said it would, people began to get the idea that this was, maybe, serious.

As a result, several new wars broke out in the Middle East, and a couple in Europe, and the End of Days Militia made its famous stand outside of Tucson and died to the last man.

There were things seen in the ocean, sometimes photographed and shown on Facebook (before they were mysteriously taken down) that didn't make much sense either. And I can tell you that not too far from us, down in Port Norris, something washed up on the beach, the size of a railroad car, with flippers but with an almost human face. I saw it myself. I stood there in the mid-day sun watching the thing melt away like wax. The newspapers said it was a whale. Then they didn't say anything.

With phone service intermittent and a national emergency declared, our failing careers seemed to have less and less to do with reality, but still Margaret and I soldiered on. By about the middle of August Margaret got a call telling her that she definitely would not be returning to her job in the fall, and on the 20th, my literary agent shot himself, so, yeah, it was a great summer.

Jackie and Caleb did what boys do, off by themselves much of the time. They seemed to be having fun.

Caleb came over a lot more often. He was around most days, at least until he and Jackie went traipsing off on their latest adventure.

One day Jackie asked me if the two of them could borrow a shovel.

"Are you going to dig up pirate treasure?" I asked him.

"Yeah, Caleb knows where there is some. Over by the Cove."

I looked over at Caleb for confirmation, but he just glanced down at his feet and wiggled his toes in the sand. He was wearing the ill-fitting tank top again that day, and it struck me that for all the tank top didn't cover much of anything, he was still almost impossibly pale, but he didn't have sunburn either. There was something odd about his eyes. They seemed about to pop out of his face.

But I didn't say anything and just gave them the shovel. Off they went, and very much to my surprise, they *found* something. I won't say they unearthed an old-fashioned sea chest, but when they came back they'd converted Jackie's t-shirt into a sack by tying the sleeves together; and when they dumped the haul out onto our kitchen table, it thumped heavily, and, God damn it, really looked like gold. Margaret protested as sand and pebbles rattled onto her clean floor, but she was as quiet as was I when she stared at the gleaming heap of strange jewelry and a misshapen crown of some sort and dozens of what might have been coins, though they were irregular in shape and the size of large cookies, and stamped with what might have been swirling tentacles.

Caleb rummaged among the pile and selected a pedant that looked a bit like a fish and partially like a man. It was on a thin chain. He put it around his neck.

"This is all I need," he said. "You can have the rest."

Jackie found another such pendant and put it on. Margaret only gaped at the two of them, speechless. Then they went outside like nothing had happened, and were just boys again, and I think they spent much of the night on the porch swing, reading manga comics by the porch light.

I swept the rest of the gold into a cardboard box. Judging by its weight, I did not doubt that it really was gold. I couldn't imagine where it had actually come from.

"Well, this ought to alleviate our financial worries for a while," I said, and the look Margaret gave me indicated that she knew as well as I did just how stupid that sounded.

* * * *

But even stupidity may contain its own nuggets of wisdom, or turn out to be prophetic, because only a few days later there was a "completely unprecedented" earthquake in eastern Pennsylvania, and the earth swallowed up a good deal of Philadelphia, even the high parts in the Northeast, which were definitely above the fall line. When a neighbor finally got through to my cell phone he said our house was gone. There was nothing worth salvaging. "Just a smoking hole in the ground," is what he said.

So we were going to have to stay down at the Shore beyond Labor Day. We registered Jackie in the local school, and he started to attend. Caleb was not in his class, or there at all.

Then there came the cold night in October when the power went out for good.

Jackie let out a yell. "Dad! Can you fix it?"

I went and checked the circuit-breakers, but no, I could not fix it. The phone was dead too. I tried my cell. No signal.

I couldn't fix it. Nobody could.

So there were the two of them, sitting alone in the dark in the TV room, and I tried to tell myself it was only my imagination that Caleb's eyes seemed unnaturally wide and faintly luminous.

Then the sounds came. That was also the first night of the Boomers or the Voices from the Sea or the Heralds of the Apocalypse, or whatever you want to call them.

At first I thought it was a ship's horn, then a fog horn, then several fog-horns. Caleb got up. He led Jackie by the hand. Margaret and I could only follow the two of them out into the darkness, down to the beach. It was still raining, and there was sleet in it. Caleb led us all. He'd kicked off the fluffy slippers and discarded the bathrobe, but, still wearing my sweat shirt and running pants, he stood in the surf, gazing out to sea, where, in the otherwise impenetrable gloom, lights began to appear; like spheres rising out of the black water, like moons, I thought, no, like eyes, opening. From out of that darkness and distance, from those glowing whatever-they-were came the sounds, a deep and thunderous booming at first, but then the notes began to modulate and they became a kind of song, which Caleb *answered*, making whistling and howling and screeching sounds that I swear no human throat has ever made.

Jackie tried to imitate him, but his own was a little boy's voice, and the result was a series of yelps, barks, and squeals.

And Caleb said to him, "It's the Call. I told you it would come." He still held Jackie by the hand and started to lead him deeper into the water.

It was Margaret who actually had the nerve to do something. You might say she had the balls in the family. She was the one who rushed forward, yanked Jackie away, and said, "No you don't! You're coming home right now!"

"But it's the Call, Mom!"

"I don't care if it's fucking Santa Claus," she said under her breath, and hauled him, squalling and protesting, up the beach and back toward our house.

Caleb turned to face me, waist-deep in the water. His eyes were definitely luminous now, like those things far out to sea.

I wanted to demand of him the truth, who he was and why he had come into our lives, and, more to the point, *what* he was.

But I didn't. I don't give myself any credit, but I think it did take a certain amount of courage to confront him at all.

All I said was, "Go away, Caleb. Leave us alone. Don't come to our house anymore. Don't play with Jackie."

He said nothing. He sank down into the water. He must have been swimming.

* * * *

That of course solved nothing. It wasn't hard to predict what happened next. One night Margaret caught Jackie at the window, leaning out into the dark, trying to make those sounds, and, in the distance, something answered him.

She was really afraid now. I could tell that. This brought us together. You know that little drawer deep inside my brain, in which I kept what was left of my love for my family? It creaked open, just a bit. I didn't argue when Margaret insisted that Jackie start sleeping in the same bed with us again. None of this "He's a big boy" crap. I knew what she meant and what she felt. I was afraid too.

During the days we just sat around the house. There was no use going out. Such neighbors as we had didn't know anything. If the government was making any rescue efforts, they weren't doing it here. Power did not come back on. The phones didn't work. The sky was filled with strange auroral effects, even in the daytime. Margaret tried to read. Believe it or not, I actually wrote a good scene in my much delayed novel-in-progress. Jackie pretended to do school work.

But there inevitably came a night when Jackie slipped out of bed as if he had to go to the bathroom, and it was maybe as much as an hour later before I was suddenly wide awake, my heart racing, and I realized that he was gone. I got up. I took the flashlight we kept by the bed and searched the house. The back door was unlocked. No further explanation necessary.

Margaret was up by then too, weeping.

I tried to play the hero. I told her I would find our boy and bring him back.

Now a hero has to have a weapon, so I rummaged around until I found a small hatchet we sometimes used for firewood. That would have to do. It was cold that night, almost winter. I put on a winter coat and fisherman's boots in case I had to do any wading, and, hatchet and flashlight in hand, I sallied forth.

The night was moonless, but brilliant with starlight and the auroras. The stars *did* ripple, like painted dots on a black cloth caught in a wild wind. The surf pounded. The Boomers, far out at sea, sang.

I made my way northward along the shoreline, the way Caleb had always gone. I knew where I was going. At Dead Man's Cove the tide was high, and the waves breaking in towers of spray. I had to make my way around the landward side, which must have taken nearly an hour. Then I trudged on and on until I came to an ancient ruin of a house, sagging to one side, as if the wind had nearly blown it over.

I didn't have any doubt where I was, whose house this was. I pushed the front door open without bothering to knock, and probed inside with the flashlight. If anybody was home, well, that was what the hatchet was for. No one seemed to be.

The first thing I noticed, inside, was the smell. For all the wind whistled through gaps in the walls, the air inside was close and stank of death and decay. When I found my way into what must have been the kitchen, I understood why. There, spread out on the floor, was the remains of a large dog, just skin and scattered bones, like what's left over when you've eaten a bony fish and scraped all the meat out.

And in the living room I found the very similar remains of what was clearly a human being.

Beyond that was a small room off to the side. Here a bare, broken up mattress lay on the muddy, sand-tracked floor. But next to that, nearly folded in a cardboard box, were a couple pairs of cut-off jeans that I certainly recognized, and a tank top, and my old Philadelphia Phillies t-shirt. This had been Caleb's room. He had definitely lived here. Next to the clothes was another box filled with manga and comic books that Jackie had no doubt given him.

There was no sense searching further. In the living room, near to the flayed man, a dozen or so books, some of them quite old-looking and quite thick, lay piled on a broken table. There were also a few flyers and leaflets. I could make out the words ESOTERIC ORDER with the flashlight. It was only some while later that I returned to the house and took some of those books and read the ones I could. Some were in languages I could not even begin to identify.

I found Caleb waiting for me back at the Cove. He stood waist-deep in the frigid water, naked. Behind him, a fog was coming in. The Boomers or Heralds or whatever they were still sounded, but their light was little more than a soft blur. The surf was quiet. The tide was going out.

I could see that the Caleb had begun to change. I can't really say how he looked. He was still as skinny and pale as ever, but most of his hair, which had never been very thick start with, was gone. He looked a bit like an old man with bulging eyes, or maybe like some long-limbed, aquatic insect.

He was sobbing. A very human sound. He held my son's limp body in his arms.

I did not have to ask to realize that Jackie was dead, drowned. He was not naked. He was wearing, absurdly, swimming trunks.

"I'm sorry," Caleb said. His voice was that polite, little boy's voice again. "I thought I could take him with me. Only those who change and answer the Call can live. That's what our deacon says. I thought Jackie could come too."

He waded slowly forward, as if to hand Jackie's body over to me. I could see then that Caleb's fingers had mutated into claws, and there was webbing between them, and the sides of his neck expanded and contracted rhythmically. He had rudimentary gills.

Well I didn't care if he was sorry or what his deacon had said, and if I'd had a gun I would have shot him right there. Instead I hurled the hatchet into his face with all my strength. Hit him too. I think the blade only glanced off, but it left a big gash on his forehead. There was blood all over his face, rather shockingly (to me at least) bright red. Then he was gone, and these was nothing left to do but haul my son's body out of the water and take him home and bury him.

* * * *

Not much more to tell. We are living, I have concluded from reading what I could of the books from the old Hutchison place, at the end of days. Other people seem to agree. Once it occurred to me that even if our power was out, it still should be possible for me to turn on the car's ignition and then use the radio. I searched the dial. I found only one station, on which a certain crazed preacher and wannabe presidential candidate was saying that God had visited his wrath upon us because we had tolerated gay marriage, and Jesus wanted us to kill all the homos. I flicked it off. I certainly didn't want to spend my last days listening to that asshole. I'd rather come to my own conclusions.

It's mostly dark now. A darkness has fallen upon the world. I am not sure the sun still rises. My wife Margaret disappeared into the darkness. I heard her screaming, and something like a black trash bag with wings had fastened itself over her face, and after a while she wasn't screaming anymore, and several more of those things attached themselves to her and carried her off into the air.

I still haven't entirely figured Caleb out. Was he really my son's best friend? Was he as much caught up in the inexorable current of events as the rest of us? I gather from my reading, particularly from a celebrated account of the Great Persecution of 1927, that his kind tend toward a heavy, squat build. So was he some kind of hormonally-deficient freak, a throwback to the more human part of his ancestry, or was he just too young, the Call forcing him through changes he wasn't ready for?

There are no answers. It doesn't matter. I cannot hear the Call now myself, but I have dreams of vast cities under the sea, and of an island emerging into gray daylight amid heaving seas, and of vast potency stirring in the darkness of a tomb.

A Wizard's Daughter
(for Asenath, at last)

by Ann K. Schwader

A wizard's daughter is a foredoomed child.
Denied the recognition of her sire
whose vision cannot scry beyond the form
of female, she must magnify her will
while passing for a mirror of his wisdom
solely. Innocent of mother-blood

to all appearances, she mingles blood
with ink, begins her training as the child
of shadows manifest. Forbidden wisdom
comes easiest: the birth-gift of a sire
ensnared by something Other, ageless will
still interwoven with this aged form

of flesh now fading. Failing. Nature forms
the surest remedy, though even blood
is not enough to satisfy him. Will
some fragile wickerwork of woman-child
suffice a mind like his? He'd thought to sire
an heir as reliquary for dark wisdom

worked upon the world. A long life's wisdom
cannot compress itself so; surely form
corrupts its function. Far too late to sire
another: he must make the most of blood
blighted by strange bargaining. This child
is his alone, last testament & will

bequeathed to no one—yet her infant will
resists. Delivered by a mother's wisdom
both alien & unsuspected, child
no longer, it assumes its proper form
at last. Begins its thirsting for the blood
of her usurper. Turned aside, her sire

seduced by Otherness (that primal sire
of myth & madness) hesitates. Whose will
is this? What hybrid spirit fills this blood

& flesh he meant as vessel? Lacking wisdom
not found in books, he only sees the form
before him. Never thinks **her mother's child.**

Betrayed at first by blood, & now by wisdom
overthrown, the dying sire finds will
prevails in many forms. One was his child.

"...she was Ephraim Waite's daughter—the child of his old age by
an unknown wife who always went veiled."
—H.P. Lovecraft, **"The Thing on the Doorstep"**

The Shadow of Azathoth is your Galaxy

by DB Spitzer

Let it be known, that the creator of us all and master of us all is the great and mighty Azathoth.
It is known Azathoth is the most powerful being known, and we now exist in his shadow.
It is known all life as we know it comes from Azathoth, all other great beings are part of Azathoth.
Azathoth is massive, and Azathoth is composed of all existing matter in many dimensions. Azathoth is the space we occupy, and all matter we contact.

Lesser creatures whom live in the 4th or 3rd dimension consider Azathoth's "shadow" to be their plane of existence. Azathoth spawned, from chaotic fission his first children, massive beings of light and gas. Their children were the first beings of matter, now called "the great old ones".

Some of Azathoth's Oldest Spawn became greedy and choose to plunder matter from Azathoth's shadow. The greater creatures didn't realize that existing in lesser space would slowly trap them. Some of the trapped formed armies, some formed religions, some simply hunted, some still sit and think. They spawned civilizations, that in turn did the same, creating a chain reaction of life across Azathoth's shadow.

The rest of Azathoth's children still dance and sing within the warm embrace of Azathoth.
We all await the day Azathoth collides with Juk-Shabb, this shall be a brutal meeting.
Azathoth shall absorb Juk-Shabb, creating a new form of existence.

Everything will be new, everything old will be gone.
Everything from matter to knowledge will become obsolete, time and dimension as we know it will become nothing.

Ascend
by Mark A. Mihalko

As I look upon dominion, the murky depths surround me
The sea of life poisoned by the uninitiated
Virtuous beliefs, now forbidden
The ancient temple crumbles
Darkness and despair abound
The cult leader rises in front of the mass
His followers prostrate to the false idol
Mocking the godliness of the Great Old One
Defiling ageless texts
Alas, the Necronomicon burns.

The echoes stir the seas
Earthquakes touch the mountains; shake Innsmouth
Voices join the chorus of thunder
Lightning dances.

Vocate ad Vetus Ones
ut resurgat
Da nobis absolutio
nos tibi cthulhu

Moloch calls, oh great and righteous one
Rise again and walk among us
The dying embers of life call to you
Your golden sanctuary tainted by the malefactors
I may not be as pious as thou art
My sins sentencing me to an eternity in exile
Yet, my faith in thy greatness never wavers
Protect me from the unrepentant
Free me from the despair
Cthulhu, I call to thee.

The shroud of Wormwood blankets the Heavens
Nemesis protrudes from the depths; Innsmouth burns
The chants illuminate the abyss
Flames purify the righteous.

Ecce coram oriri ones magna pollens
Denique, nostrae salutis adest
Cthuhlu amplectere benedicat ipse pietatis

Per vires, deficiat impiis.

As I stand over oblivion, the infidels beg for absolution
The sea of life sanctified by the blood of the martyrs
Righteous beliefs, now embraced
Prophets bow before the beasts
Idols testify before the throne
Darkness swallowed by the inferno
The golden dawn blinds the malefactors
The Great Old One ascends
The Necronomicon lives again
And, Cthulhu walks among man.

The Solace of the Farther Moon

by Allan Rozinski

We found a secret haven
on the dark side of the moon—
not on the sunny-side up,
where life is exposed by light
too bright to escape notice.

Best not to linger in the
glaring confusion of the day;
we seek out the
comfort of constant shadows
on the dark half.

On the farther moon, in the
sanctuary of our hidden world,
we can sit atop a mons
in solitude, or descend undisturbed
to the bottom of a tranquil sea.

With only the eyes of distant stars
to watch us, we hope to keep
its secrets as ours alone—
to live here concealed
under the cover of eternal night.

But we are trapped in the orbit
of that baleful blue orb that menaces
our sky; the foul odor of desperation
rises from the very rot of
humanity's self-inflicted wounds.

Their planet grows too
small, and waxes most apocalyptic.

We fear for our future then: another
celestial body to be ravaged,
bored through and hollowed
out by alien worms
savaging fruit without defense.

The Stars Are Always Right

or, The Evening Not Nice

by Charles Lovecraft

It seems the stars are always right.
I look out of my window, bright
With constellations of all kind,
But something strikes my deeper mind.

I see a tilting of Time's dots,
A drawing back of ancient spots,
As if a mighty travesty
Were wheeling here to flex so free.

And I recoil as if a spark
Galvanic, charged from eons' dark,
Had reached out from the hedging gulfs,
All edging closer like perched wolfs,

And leaned into my lonely room,
A hand of weirdness from the gloom,
That clutches at my throat and heart,
While chills throughout my cold blood dart,

To see the glances of the spheres,
Shift wryly in their churning fears,
Like curtains on a stage of dark,
Which bring the changes that they mark.

The night scapes, bending in their spree,
Freewheeling in weird majesty,
Depart from spheres unknown and black
And reach our eyes in dark attack.

And I stand empty of all grief,
In illimitable relief,
Awaiting on the sounds that come
To blot life out and darkly numb.

The mulling eons and their eyes,
That sift down from the frightened skies,
Serve here beneath the R'lyehan waves
The alien monster of our graves.

Daemonic Nathicana
by K.A. Opperman

I watched as divine Nathicana
Returned to the garden of Zaïs,
The zephyr-lulled garden of Zaïs,
Where lounges the lazy iguana.
I watched her descend to her dais,
Her pink-stoned and sphinx-holden dais,
Daemonic, encrimsoned with mana,
The queenly, the cold Nathicana.

She bore on her brow red Banapis,
A crescent like horns of a daemon,
A sinful and star-fallen daemon
With eyes like deep pools of black lapis.
I longed for my long-ago leman,
In yesteryear's labyrinth my leman,
A man who knows not where his map is,
Bewildered 'neath blood red Banapis.

She walked on the breath blown from Yabon,
Did ebony-tressed Nathicana,
The scarlet-mouthed whore Nathicana,
At autumn, the day men call Mabon.
And over the flora and fauna—
Marmoreal flora and fauna—
She shed ruby light that looked drab on
Fair Zaïs, 'neath Dzannin-cursed Yabon.

ALLEN K '17

Asenath

by Ashley Dioses

Her eyes, her strangely large and gleaming eyes, were dark
Against her gorgeous face and yet she left her mark
In Arkham when she met her lover. Then her claws
Sunk deep into her prey, while hiding all her flaws.
She was one of the Innsmouth Waites, from the seaport
Of such repute, infamous for the strangest sort
Of dwellers that live in the half-deserted town.
Her name was Asenath, she-devil of such renown.

At Miskatonic, she, magician, ruled the school—
Accomplishing such marvels to the eyes of fools.
Asenath professed the ability to raise storms,
And animals, beloved pets, would not, to her, warm.
She could make canines howl with motions of her hand
And then displayed, at times, remnants of knowledge banned
Or languages so singular they shocked her mates.
With winks, she would extract some facts from altered states.
She was a hypnotist and, without any shame,
She would swap forms to be free from physical frames.

By gazing at a fellow student she'd exchange
Her personality with theirs to just derange
Those so-called weaker minds and practice all her skills.
Her husband, she ensnared, was just right for her thrills.
She eyed him with a predatory air, for she
Desired his mind, his fine-wrought brain, to become free
From Asenath's current form and gain a body near
Her form as Kamog, once a wizard that struck fear.

Her husband spoke of hideous exchanges of
Her mind, while his body summoned spirits above,
Below, and between from a Cyclopean waste.
He felt he was becoming gradually erased.
Asenath lay felled, by his own hand, in their storeroom,
Yet little did he know that that would be his doom!
She switched her mind with his while he was locked away
In Arkham Sanitarium where she would stay.
Asenath was dead so long ago for it was Fate
That would reveal she was, her father, Ephrem Waite!

The Book of Eibon/ Le Livre D'eibon

"Sfatlicllp"

trans. by Frederick J. Mayer

Time is figuretively ripe
Beauty true is bold Sfatlicllp image
of the socket grotto grotesque erotica
soulfulful windows arabesque dreams vintage
She possesses acute teeth vagina dentata
revealing experiences in blood storage
making one so nervous nurturing Nirvana
When the Tiger Smoked the Pipe: 1

Timeless hashish-eater eyes
forbidden bale encrusted nuptial
kinship fantastque grande pere Tsathoggua
Shathak mate nonanthropomorphical
inner courses of black spleen Zvilpoghua
ejaculation child, sire supernal
begining birthing dimension dementia
Then cosmique grand mal disquise

Timing depth climb downward cave
Voormis Venus sought akin pilgrimage
"Hyperborea beyond Hyperborea"; 2
Behold Her obstreperous passage
obscene statuesque erogenous zone vulva
bestial in furs stone site lineage
death clime ceases love is molten goddess a
Figure carnal worship crave

Timescape of stars are right type
impassion pas de deux ebon marriage
bestiaire d'amour pregnant noir curiosa
Noctuary aphrodisiaque page
Rapture Fin de siecle whorls Massa damnata